Ghosts
of the
Titanic

Ghosts of the Titanic

JULIE LAWSON

Holiday House / New York

1   3   5   7   9   10   8   6   4   2

Library of Congress Cataloging-in-Publication Data

Lawson, Julie, 1947–
Ghosts of the Titanic / by Julie Lawson.
p. cm.
Summary: Alternates between the tales of Angus Seaton, the youngest crew member on a boat
recovering bodies from the Titanic wreckage in 1912, and Kevin Messenger, a modern-day class
clown in Victoria, British Columbia, who helps lay a victim's spirit to rest.
ISBN 978-0-8234-2423-8 (hardcover)
[1. Supernatural—Fiction.   2. Titanic (Steamship)—Fiction.   3. Shipwrecks—Fiction.
4. Identity—Fiction.   5. Ghosts—Fiction.   6. Conduct of life—Fiction.   7. Family life—
British Columbia—Fiction.   8. Victoria (B.C.)—Fiction.   9. Nova Scotia—Fiction.]   I. Title.
PZ7.L43828Gho 2012
[Fic]—dc23
2011037867

For Steph,
Steve, and Piper

Prologue

The ghost was waiting on the water.

What have you done?

What has become of my precious boy?

The man in the dory was not surprised. He had come to know the ghost and her endless questions.

"He's dead like all the others." The man was weary of her questions, weary beyond imagining.

Has his body been taken by the sea?

Does he weep for me in the deep?

Does he walk on land, searching for me?

"I saw him buried. I put roses on his casket."

How will he know me? How will he know me?

He wept for her and her lost child. He wept for his own.

Come with me, robber of the dead.

Come back and undo what you have done.

Come with me . . .

He longed to go, but it was too soon. She was the albatross around his neck, his guilty conscience. She was the penance he had to pay.

What have you done? Thief of a lost boy's past . . .

He turned the boat around and rowed for shore, hearing her voice in every lap of the oars.

Daybreak, April 21, 1912

Bodies, bodies everywhere. Bodies rolling on the blue-black sea, faceup in the drift ice, nudging and bobbing against the wreckage, against the cutters of the men sent out to recover them. Ordinary Seaman Angus Seaton was the youngest of those men, and the task was hitting him hard.

They'd come upon the first signs of the *Titanic* disaster the previous day. An overturned lifeboat, deck chairs, silver flasks, cushions, gloves, the wadding from life belts, bits of tattered clothing—miles and miles of floating debris. They'd expected to reach the disaster site that same evening, but fog and ice had slowed their progress, forcing them to stop and let the ship drift overnight.

At first light they'd taken their positions on deck, watchful and silent, their eyes scouring the sea for any sign of a human form.

Angus watched from the fo'c'sle deck, steeling himself for the job ahead. The sooner they got started, the sooner it would be over and, no matter how gruesome, it was better to recover the bodies and bury them properly than to leave them floating about for weeks.

A sudden shout from the wing deck. "Up ahead to starboard!"

Angus had spotted it, too. Way off in the distance, a cluster of white flecks, rising and falling with the rise and fall of the waves. Gulls. A sight he'd seen a thousand times. A large flock of gulls, resting on the water.

The others thought the same, even Captain Larnder and the officers on the bridge. Until they'd gotten closer and realized that the white flecks were not gulls but the tops of life belts. Each one holding up a body. Bodies by the hundreds.

Bodies, bodies everywhere . . .

Chapter One

Victoria, British Columbia

"Halifax?" Kevin burst into the kitchen. "No way I'm going to Halifax!"

"Hello to you, too," his mother said. "How did things go at the pool?"

"Fine. Everything was fine until now." He shot her a look, half-noticed his father chopping something at the counter, and, after elbowing past Courtney to open the fridge door, he continued to rant. "No way I'm going to Halifax—it's the other side of the country. Forget it! I'm not leaving my friends, and me and Zack have got plans. Swimming lessons, remember? I'm already behind Zack, thanks to soccer. You can't make me go to Halifax, you know. I've got rights. I'll move in with Zack or something. No *way* I'm moving to Halifax."

Kevin stopped rummaging through the fridge long enough to toss back a handful of grapes and gulp down some chocolate milk from the carton. "Whose idea was this, anyway? Courtney's, I bet. You want to visit the little house of Green Gables or something, Courtney? Hey! Isn't anybody listening?" He shut the fridge door and turned to see what they were up to.

What? They were laughing at him. His sister was practically doubled over, his mum was chuckling, his dad's shoulders were shaking over a pile of red and green peppers—at least he was in a good mood for once. "What's so funny? I'm just stating an opinion."

"We're not *moving,* you goof," Courtney said.

Kevin frowned. "I heard you."

"You heard a bit of talk," his mum said. "And instead of asking about it, you come barging in—"

"And jump to conclusions," Courtney interrupted. "And just so you know, Green Gables is on Prince Edward Island, not Nova Scotia."

"Think for a minute," his dad said. "Why would we move to Halifax?"

"What're you saying now?"

"Oh Kevin." His mother gave an exasperated sigh. "Wash up and set the table. Supper's almost ready."

He grabbed a chocolate sandwich cookie and made for the door, only to hear his dad say, "But just because we're not moving to Halifax doesn't mean we're not going."

What was that supposed to mean?

It became clear at supper—sort of. "Let me get this straight," Kevin said, reviewing what his dad had told them. "A letter comes in the mail. By courier. So it's important. And it's from some lawyer in Halifax and he tells you that you've inherited a mansion."

"He doesn't say it's a mansion. Only a large piece of waterfront property with a house on it."

"Okay. But you've never heard of the place, you don't know anybody who lives in Nova Scotia, and the guy who left it to you, this Angus Seaton, you've never heard of him, either? Whoo!" he said, shaking his head. "Am I missing something? This is too weird."

"But isn't it great?" said Courtney. "Aren't you excited? It's like winning the lottery. I can't wait to see it."

"How do we know the letter's not from one of those scammers from Nigeria or somewhere?"

"Because the letter doesn't start with 'Dearest' or 'Dear One' and nobody's asking for a bank account number," his mum said. "Don't worry, it's all aboveboard. Your dad's already talked to the lawyer, and next week he's going to Nova Scotia to have a look."

"You are, Dad? Is that what you guys were talking about?"

"Partly. I've booked a flight, and the lawyer's going to introduce me to the property manager and show me around the place." He consulted the letter. "It's called Shearwater Point, on the south shore of Nova Scotia, a couple of hours outside Halifax. Right on the coast."

"It's waterfront, so it's got its own beach? Cool! And we get to miss school?"

"Changed your mind already?" Courtney said. "A minute ago you didn't want to leave your friends."

"Sorry, Kevin," his dad said. "Nobody's missing school. I'm going to check out the situation and then we'll see."

"Are you going to find out who this Seaton guy was?" Kevin asked. The whole business was creepy. "You should go on the Internet. That's the first thing I would have done."

"I did. There are a few listings under *Angus Seaton*, but none of them fit."

"A real-life mystery," said Kevin. He could write about it in Language Arts. Not yet, though. Not until he had some answers. Number one, who was Angus Seaton?

Chapter Two

Kevin couldn't get the question out of his mind.

Good thing he'd done his homework early in the weekend, instead of waiting till the last minute. Otherwise he never would have finished. No problem, though. His science project, "The Iceberg that Sank the *Titanic*," was in his backpack and ready to be delivered. On time. Ms. Ratchet would be stunned.

So who was Angus Seaton? How was he connected to Dad? Kevin mulled over the questions as he was biking to school, but the ideas he came up with were too far-fetched to be believable.

Meanwhile, it was another Monday. Another week "on board the sinking ship." He entered the classroom, pausing to examine the gigantic floor-to-ceiling iceberg the class had made out of papier mâché. Good thing their *Titanic* studies were coming to an end, as it was beginning to look grungy. Somebody was chipping at it, peeling away loose bits of paper. Spring melt, in a way. The red line Kevin had added still looked good, if he did say so himself. It was an important addition, too. You couldn't have the iceberg without showing where the *Titanic*'s paint had rubbed off during the collision.

Titanic: The Artifact Exhibition was the biggest deal of the century, the way Ms. Ratchet was going on about it. Not only had she organized a class field trip to the museum to see the exhibit, she had planned every lesson for the past two months around a *Titanic* theme. In Science, they were studying the properties of water, particularly water in its solid state (as in icebergs). In Art, they were creating large-scale dioramas to show the *Titanic* at sea (with icebergs). In Social Studies, it was the class system of the time, and how it was reflected on board the ship. In Language Arts, they were putting on a "You Were There" television program in which a "host" interviewed a *Titanic* "survivor." This involved a lot of research and, in the case of Kevin's partner, Natalie, an embarrassing amount of sobbing. Playing a survivor who'd lost her husband and son, Natalie insisted on breaking down in order to make the scene "more heart-wrenching."

In Music, they had learned some of the popular tunes that the ship's band had played during the voyage, and now they were about to learn a song written after the disaster.

"'Oh, They Built the Ship *Titanic*,'" Kevin called out, pleased that he recognized the title on the song sheet. "We did this in third grade. Remember, you guys, in Ms. Livesay's class?" Before he could stop himself, he started to sing. "'Oh it was sad, so sad, it was sad, so sad, it was sad when the great ship went down to the bottom—'"

"Kevin!" Ms. Ratchet cut in. "Would you like to teach the song?"

"Sure!"

He knew at once that he'd done it again, called her bluff instead of backing down. The way her mouth tightened and her eyes narrowed—only for a second, but man, if looks could kill.

Too late for her to back down, too, the way the class was reacting. The cheers and applause as Kevin made his way to the front of the class—heck, he might as well make the most of it. A maestro's bow (repeated several times). Arms up, for attention. "I'll sing a line and you guys repeat it, okay?" He cleared his throat. "'Oh they built the ship *Titanic* to sail the oceans blue.' Now it's your turn. Ready?" He led them in, but a tickle in his throat turned into a giggle and before long he was laughing so hard he couldn't continue, not with the other kids laughing, singing, and talking, not with Hannah and her clones competing as to who could "shush" the loudest, and Natalie warning they'd get a detention.

Ms. Ratchet's voice finally broke through the clamor. "Kevin! Sit down." Instant silence. "How many times do I have to tell you?"

"I never heard you the first time," he said, and right away wished he hadn't. Why couldn't he keep his mouth shut? Once he made that first move, he never knew when to stop.

"You can hear me now. Sit down!"

"But you said—"

"*Sit down!*" Grabbing him by the elbow, Ms. Ratchet pushed him toward his desk.

"Hey, you can't do that, get your hands off me."

"I've had it. You think I'm going to put up with your behavior? Time and time again—"

"I never did anything." Kevin shrugged her off as he reached his desk, risked a smirk in Zack's direction.

"That's *it*, Kevin! You think this is funny? Get out!"

"But you just—"

"GET OUT!"

Sighing loudly, he left the room. Sheesh! The little kids down the hall would be peeing themselves after hearing Ms. Ratchet shout like that. She could do permanent damage to her vocal cords. She could be hoarse for days. Ha! She'd be begging Kevin to teach the song.

He put his ear to the door. Nothing. They weren't singing. Ms. Ratchet was probably waiting for her heart to slow down, or for her vocal cords to repair themselves. A temper like that—whoa, it was as bad as Dad's. Did she have high blood pressure like him, too?

He hummed the *Titanic* song under his breath. He'd always liked it, remembered every word of every verse—and there were a lot of verses. *Little children wept and cried as the waves swept o'er the side...*

Time for a washroom break.

He sauntered down the hall, pausing to look at the displays of class artwork. Anything by Kevin? Nope. Better luck next month.

He returned to his spot outside the classroom door and listened again. What was going on in there? Was he missing anything? He put his hand on the doorknob. If he turned it real slow—

"Good morning, Kevin."

He jumped back, startled. "Oh hi, Mr. Driscoll."

"What are you doing out here?"

"Nothing."

"I can see that. Well?"

Kevin shrugged, staring at the scuffed toes of his sneakers.

"How about coming into my office? I'll give you some paper and you can write about what you've done this time. How's Courtney, by the way? I hear she's the star of the Vic High soccer team."

"Yeah." Kevin traipsed after the principal, glaring into his back. Cripes. Weren't things bad enough without Courtney coming into it?

"Have a seat," Mr. Driscoll said, nodding at a desk in the corner. He handed Kevin a pencil and a stack of paper.

"Do I have to use all this paper?"

"Depends on how much of an apology you need to make."

"A Post-it note, then," he mumbled.

"What's that?"

"Nothing."

Dear Ms. Ratchet, I'm sorry . . .

He paused. Well, if Mr. Driscoll wanted him to apologize, he'd be the star of apologies. He'd spoken a zillion "sorries" in his seventh-grade year, but had never actually written an apology.

He used words like *irresponsible, arrogant, disrespectful*. He promised he would behave *in a manner befitting a seventh-grade boy on the cusp of adulthood*. (He took pride in that sentence.) He apologized for not following his sister's example, even though Ms. Ratchet hadn't taught Courtney, and said it was difficult living in her shadow. He apologized for making the other kids laugh (even though he hadn't done it on purpose), especially during a song about a whole lot of people dying. He ended the letter by begging her to accept his apology, and swearing that he'd behave for the remaining six weeks of school.

He read over the letter and almost gagged. Had he actually written that stuff? He'd laid it on too thick. Especially the part where he said he was sorry if he'd made her first year of teaching a nightmare, because he actually liked being in her class. It was interesting and fun.

She'd never believe it. He'd be worse off than before.

As an afterthought, he added that his dad had gotten some unexpected news and it had thrown everybody into a turmoil. So Kevin had been awake all night, and that accounted for his attitude.

"Finished, Kevin? Let's have a look."

Kevin drummed his fingers on the desk, waiting for the verdict.

"That's quite a piece of writing," Mr. Driscoll said after reading it. "Ms. Ratchet will be pleased."

It was too much to hope for, getting off with a measly letter, so Kevin's after-school detention didn't come as a total surprise. "Can I do my homework?" he said. "Or do I have to write lines?"

"Neither," said Ms. Ratchet, putting a mark on the board. "You can stare at this dot and think for twenty minutes. Then we'll have a chat."

He groaned silently and focused on the dot, wondering if it would put him into a trance. Was she playing some weird mind trick on him? What was there to think about? What he'd said in the letter was pretty truthful, mostly, even though he had gotten carried away. Some of the stuff he'd written? If any of his friends got hold of that letter he'd be classed as a "Natalie" for the rest of his life.

Six weeks of school . . . how hard would it be to act like a kid on the cusp of adulthood? Kevin Messenger, star of—what was the expression?—turning over a new leaf.

When his time was up—had it been twenty minutes or did Ms. Ratchet want to get some more coffee?—she called him to her desk and thanked him for his letter. "Things would go much better for you if you didn't act like such a clown," she said. "And you've got to stop talking back. It's rude and disruptive. There are other ways of getting attention. Am I right?" Her eyes demanded an answer.

"Yes." He winced.

"Kevin . . . are things going well at home?"

"Huh?" What kind of question was that?

"In your letter you mentioned some unexpected news."

"Oh, but it's good news, don't worry. I can't talk about it, though."

"Okay, I understand. And Courtney. Do you get along with your sister?"

"Yeah, sure."

"That's good to hear. It can be tough sometimes, having an older brother or sister. Anyway, Kevin, I accept your apology. But you remember what I said on Friday?"

He nodded. "Three strikes and I miss the field trip."

"That's right. You've got two strikes left. It's up to you."

"I'm planning to turn over a new leaf."

"Good," she said.

"It's something my dad's always on about."

She smiled. "I'll see you tomorrow, then. If I recognize you."

"Huh?"

"Joke, Kevin. Since you're turning over a new leaf?"

"Oh, I get it." He gave a little laugh and left quickly, before she got too smiley or told any more dumb jokes.

"Blue ice!" Kevin announced at supper that night. "Anybody know what that is?" He helped himself to some mashed potatoes, enjoying the way he'd broken the usual supper routine. For once he was the first to bring up a subject.

Kevin couldn't remember when the routine started. His parents had said it was after they'd been to some teachers' conference and heard that kids generally did better in school when the whole family ate supper together and talked. Not *arguing* talk, but meaningful talk. Like telling stories, exchanging news, discussing plans. Or being on the hot seat answering inane questions. *What did you learn in school today, Kevin?*

Nothing.

Not tonight. He looked up from buttering his potatoes and saw that he had their attention. With any luck, he might get through an entire meal without having to hear the irritating details of Courtney's day.

"Well," he began. "You know the *Titanic*? The reason it hit the iceberg was because they didn't see it until it was too late. And you know why they didn't see it? I'll tell you. You see, you get these glaciers calving—that means they break off into icebergs—and these icebergs float in the current, and they're in the sun and they start to melt on top and after a while they flip over. So what used to be at the bottom is now on the surface of the water, see?" He picked up the bottle of salad dressing and flipped it over to demonstrate (cap on—thank God, since he hadn't checked). "The part that was underwater is dark blue because of the seawater, and when it's on top it's really hard to see at night. Get it? Hey, don't take all the potatoes, Courtney. I want some more. And the night the *Titanic* sunk...sank— whatever—it was way calm, so there weren't any waves breaking against the iceberg. If there *had* been, the lookouts would've seen the white froth. See? Any more chicken, Mum? I'm still hungry.

"And the lookout guy, his name was Frederick Fleet, he was up in the crow's nest, right? But he didn't have binoculars, so when he saw it, *bam!* Too late. He said it was as high as the crow's nest, that's about fifty feet above the deck. And get this. He sent a message to the bridge—*iceberg dead ahead,* or something—and thirty-seven seconds later they hit it. Thirty-seven seconds! Can you believe it? So. Ask me anything."

He could always count on his mum. She and Courtney got right into it while he was finishing his dinner. They asked on-topic questions, too, like they were really interested.

"How about you, Dad? Any questions?"

"How was soccer practice?"

"Dad! Aren't you interested in the *Titanic*?"

"Up to a point."

"It's fascinating, Kevin," his mum said. "You seem to be enjoying it."

"It's a disaster. What can I say? Anyhow, I did my science report on the iceberg and the damage it caused—you know, it didn't cut a big gash in the hull like everybody thought—and I actually did an extra report on icebergs in the North Atlantic between 1900 and 1912. And tomorrow I have to talk about it on *Science Wizards*. That's our pretend TV show, and Zack is the cameraman and gets to record it. Ms. Ratchet says the iceberg's like a character in the story, it's so, I dunno, larger than life. Whew!" He paused for breath. "What's for dessert?"

"Chocolate truffle ice cream. Help yourself," his mum said as Kevin jumped up from the table. "Sounds like you're getting along better with Ms. Ratchet. Am I right?"

"Kevin . . ." Courtney made a face. "Stop eating it out of the carton. Put it in a bowl and give me some."

"Make that four, since you're up," said his father.

"Maybe. I guess. Getting along with Ms. Ratchet, I mean." He dished out four bowls of ice cream and brought them to the table. "The thing is—don't have a heart attack or anything—I have a plan." He leaned back in his chair, arms folded across his chest, and said proudly, "I've decided to turn over a new leaf. I even told Ms. Ratchet."

His mother smiled. "That's wonderful news. Did you hear that, Jim?"

"What's that?"

Kevin groaned. "Dad! Don't you ever listen? I'm turning over a new leaf."

"I'm glad to hear it," he said, looking up from his ice cream. "You can start off at tomorrow's soccer game. You do some practice after school today? How about you, Courtney? Big game on Saturday."

"No kidding. You going to make it?"

Kevin tuned out his dad's gung-ho response to Courtney and the blah, blah, blah that followed. Never mind that Dad had asked him a question without waiting for an answer. Just as well, since Kevin hadn't gone to practice and he'd totally forgotten tomorrow's game. Stupid soccer.

He looked at his dad and sister, at it again. Gym teacher, coach, and former soccer champ Jim Messenger and star player Captain Courtney, going on about scores, saves, competitions, tournaments, provincial finals, whatever.

"C'mon, Kev," his mother said, catching his eye. "Let's double-check the Internet for Angus Seaton. Your dad might have missed something."

"Yeah," Kevin laughed. "Or gotten sidetracked by you-know-what."

Chapter Three

"Yay, team!" Kevin yelled from his place as goalie. The Cougars had scored another goal, bringing the game to a tie. He hoped they'd break the tie, if only to keep the play at that end of the field.

He didn't mind being goalie. Coach Salter had told him it was because he was the tallest kid on the team and could stretch out the farthest, but Kevin knew the real reasons. First, because everyone else hated being goalie (too boring), and second, because Kevin was worse at all the other positions. He was a good kicker, but kicking wasn't exactly a position.

The best part of being goalie was being able to laze around in the goal area and think about the things he'd rather be doing. Like swimming with Zack at the Crystal Pool. The worst part was when he had to pay attention and keep the other team from scoring.

Today's game against the Orcas was going well. It was almost over, too—not only the game, but soccer and school. In another six weeks he could get back to swimming lessons. And if he worked at his crawl and backstroke he could pass Level Seven and move up to Level Eight with Zack. Unless Dad decided they were going to Nova Scotia—

"Kevin, wake up!" The angry shout jolted him back to the game.

"Oh, God," he muttered. Just what he was afraid of. The Orcas were on the attack. The ball was overhead and about to land in the goal zone. The only way to stop it was to leap up and head it—but it was coming so hard and fast Kevin panicked and jumped out of the way. He didn't think twice, he just did it.

Game over. Cougars 10, Orcas 11.

Coach Salter made no effort to hide his disappointment. "What's the matter with you, Kevin? The most crucial part of the game and you let us down. Again. Why can't you pay attention? And why weren't you at practice yesterday? If it weren't for your—never mind." He slapped Kevin on the back. "Go on, get changed. Practice tomorrow."

Kevin trudged across the field, dreading the locker-room scene. He knew what Coach Salter was thinking. *If it weren't for your dad.* Yeah. If it weren't for Coach Jim, buddy of all coaches, Kevin wouldn't be on the team in the first place. Why didn't he just up and quit? Well, maybe he would. Quitting soccer could be part of his new-leaf turnover. Save Coach Salter the trouble of kicking him off.

The jibes started the minute he walked into the locker room.

"You play like a girl, Messenger. Oooh, I might hurt my little head."

"Worse than a girl. Ever see his sister play? Courtney's awesome."

"What, you watch girls' soccer?"

"My sister's on the high school team, the same as Courtney."

"Look, Messenger. The point is, you can't be afraid of the ball."

"I'm not afraid. It was a mistake, okay? And leave my sister out of it."

News traveled fast. Kevin had barely sat down for supper before his dad said, "I heard about the game."

Kevin sighed. What did Coach Salter do, call up Dad and tell him his wimp of a son had let the team down again? Didn't Salter have anything better to do?

"What's the matter with you? The hours we've spent practicing, coaching—"

"Wait a sec," Kevin protested. "It could have been worse. I made some good saves. Did Salter tell you that?"

His dad went on as if he hadn't heard. "The simplest thing, you manage to screw it up. What were you thinking? Can't you do anything right?"

"I made the swim team," Kevin muttered.

"What's that? Speak up."

"I made the swim team. Remember? And you made me quit 'cause it interfered with soccer?" Of all times, his voice had to crack. He got up, his face a flaming torch, and stomped out.

"Get back here. We're not finished—"

"I've had it!" Kevin yelled, and stormed outside. He was finished with soccer. Let Courtney be the soccer star. She was the star of everything else. She hadn't laughed when his voice cracked, though. He owed her for that.

He went over to the SUV parked in the driveway and scowled at the bumper sticker. *Proud Soccer Dad.* He gave it a vicious kick, wishing his shoes were muddy, wishing he had a can of spray paint to wipe out the words. Better yet, a Magic Marker to turn it into something true. *Proud Soccer Dad of Courtney, not Kevin.*

No way was he going to the soccer practice tomorrow. What was the point? He didn't have any friends on the team, and Coach Salter was a full-of-himself jock. Nope, tomorrow after school he'd hang out with Zack, go downtown and do something, *anything*, as long as it wasn't soccer.

When Kevin got home the next day he was surprised to see the SUV in the driveway. Was he that late, or was his dad home earlier than usual? He was even more surprised when Courtney met him at the door with their watch-out-for-Dad sign, a finger-slash across the throat.

"There's a message on the answering machine," she whispered. "Dad heard it before I did, otherwise I would've written it down for you and erased it. God, Kev. What did you do? Never mind," she added as Kevin brushed past without answering. "Rhetorical question."

He was on edge during dinner, his stomach in knots, waiting for the blowup, his dad playing a cat-and-mouse game, acting like everything was fine, waiting for the right moment to pounce. Courtney talked about her incredibly amazing day and, for once, Kevin hoped she'd never stop. But what was there to worry about? The message was probably from Coach Salter. *Hey, Jim. Just letting you know that Kevin's off the team. He missed another practice.* Or was Ms. Ratchet ratting on him about Monday? His behavior had been perfect since then...

"How did your practice go, Kev?"

He looked up abruptly, realizing that Courtney had stopped talking and that all eyes were on him. "Good," he said. So the message wasn't from Coach Salter. "It went good. Except my head hurts from all the heading."

"That explains it. A bump on the head, you get confused. Is that how you lost your wallet? You dropped it on the soccer field?"

"Yeah...I mean, no. What is this? I never lost my wallet. It's in my back pocket." He reached down to check. "What the—it's not there. How did that happen? Unless I took it out and forgot and left it in my room. I'll go look."

"Stay where you are. I'll tell you what happened. You skipped soccer practice, went to town, and hung around at the Bay Centre. Then you managed to lose your wallet, came home late, and lied."

"I never—"

"I left school early to go to your practice," his dad went on. "You weren't there. I came home and checked the answering machine. Guess what? There's a message for a Kevin Messenger at this address, whose wallet was found in the food court at the Bay Centre by a gentleman who'd like to return it. Your student card's in it, and about fifteen dollars. He left his name and number so you can call and arrange a time."

"Oh, man, that was lucky. What a nice guy. Can I phone him now?"

"What part was lucky, Kevin? The lying part? Missing another practice? Being careless enough to lose your wallet? Anything else we should know about?"

"Yeah, I had a detention on Monday."

"Now you're being smart."

"I am not! It's true. That's why I missed soccer."

"When are you going to grow up? Honest to God, you're the most irresponsible…What about commitment? You let everybody down—the team, the coach—and it's not only soccer. What about your schoolwork? You're not interested in anything. You don't even try."

"That's not true," Kevin protested.

"When are you going to stop clowning around and apply yourself? You want to be a loser all your life?"

"I'd rather be a loser than a—a cliché like you."

"That's enough," his mother said sharply. "Both of you, finish your supper. Kevin, you can phone about your wallet later."

"Know what, Dad? They don't care. The team, Coach Salter—they're happy when I don't show up. The only one who cares is you. It's like—oh, what's the use. *Soccer*," he spat. "It's an albatross around my neck, that's what it is."

"An albatross?" Courtney laughed. "*Cliché?* You're getting pretty literary, aren't you?"

"Shut up." Kevin drained his glass of milk, slammed the glass down, and left the table. Family time was over as far as he was concerned. If Dad had just asked him about his day, instead of going ballistic, Kevin would have said that he'd gone to the downtown public library with Zack after school, and had done another search for Angus Seaton. He'd tried different spelling variations, the Halifax telephone directory, even a couple of old-timers soccer teams in Nova Scotia. He hadn't found anything, but he might have. Dad wouldn't have called him a loser then.

"You're grounded till Monday," his dad called after him.

"Tell me something new," Kevin shouted over his shoulder. He ran to his room, taking the stairs two at a time. Good thing Dad hadn't pulled the "three strikes and you're out" rule; otherwise Kevin would be missing the field trip for sure. He'd made it at school, though. One day to go, and two strikes to spare.

Too bad he hadn't asked Mr. Driscoll to photocopy the letter of apology. He could have crossed out some of the stuff he'd written and given it to his dad. Would he have been pleased? Not likely. He hated when Kevin "blamed" Courtney. Kevin didn't blame her. It was hardly her fault their dad was a jerk. A cliché.

Cliché? What had made him say that? He wasn't sure if he'd used it the right way, but it felt good saying it. Former soccer champion turned high school gym teacher, soccer coach, and star player of old-timers soccer. And he could have gone on to play pro. How could Kevin live up to that?

Kevin called the man about the wallet and told him he could keep the money as a reward, he was so grateful. The man declined (nice!) and said he'd drop by within the hour.

After his wallet had been delivered, Kevin set his mind to homework. Seeing that Courtney's door was open, he stopped and asked if she'd ever heard of the poem "The Rime of the Ancient Mariner."

Courtney paused from rearranging the photos on her bulletin board. " 'The Ancient Mariner'? Sure. We read it last year in English Lit. 'A painted ship on a painted ocean.' It's the poem about the albatross. Nice one, by the way, what you said at supper. That, and *cliché*." She grinned.

"Yeah, well. Sorry I told you to shut up."

"You're forgiven. Does Jude's picture look better here . . . or here?"

Courtney's boyfriend of the hour. "Whatever," Kevin said. "No, put it in the center so it's hidden by your soccer trophy."

"Get out," she laughed.

"Isn't it cool?" Kevin said. "The poem, I mean. We read parts of it today. There's this ancient curse, and if a sailor kills an albatross he brings doom on his crew. So that's what happens, and the guy's forced to go around with the dead albatross hanging around his neck. Can you imagine?"

"I know. Gross."

"And every time he meets somebody, he has to tell them the story. It's like his punishment. Listen to this. 'Bodies, bodies, everywhere, and all the decks did reek—' "

"It's *water, water*, everywhere."

"Yeah, in the poem. But this is an assignment. You have to follow the pattern and make up four verses of your own, but on a different topic. Mine's about a pirate battle. Actually it's after the battle, when all the attackers are dead."

"Let's hear it."

" 'Bodies, bodies, everywhere, and all the decks did reek, Bodies, bodies, everywhere, and nobody could speak.' "

"It's a bit morbid."

"Thanks! That's the whole idea." He turned to leave. "Hey, Courtney? When's Dad going to Halifax?"

"Next Friday. He'll be gone for five days."

Five whole days. What a relief. Kevin could already feel the tension draining away.

Chapter Four

Titanic: The Artifact Exhibition was the best thing Kevin had ever seen at the museum.

"Welcome aboard!" An actor playing the part of Captain Edward Smith greeted the class as they filed up the gangway. "Welcome to the floating palace, the safest, most luxurious ship ever built."

It wasn't only actors and gallery interpreters who got to play a role. At the top of the gangway, everyone was handed a boarding card that related to an actual passenger.

"I'm Karl Skoog," Kevin said, reading his card. "Age twelve, traveling from Stockholm, Sweden, to Iron Mountain, Michigan. I boarded the *Titanic* at Southampton with my parents, one brother, and two sisters. Is anybody else a Skoog?" He waved his card at one of the interpreters. "Do I survive? I'm in third class."

"Excuse me," Hannah butted in. "Are you going to check Kevin for lice and diseases? Our teacher said all the third-class passengers had to be inspected by a doctor before they could board."

"True," the interpreter said, "but we're not taking the reality that far. Listen please, everyone. As you enter, imagine you are the person on the boarding card. You're excited, you're enjoying the experience of being on this magnificent ship, and you have no idea what's in store. At the very end of the exhibit, you'll find out your fate. All set?"

"Can I please get a different card?" Kevin asked. "This one's third class, and they didn't have much fun. Plus most of them died."

"It's not real, stupid," Natalie said. "And third-class passengers had fun. Remember that Jack guy, in the movie? He was in third class—"

"Yeah, what a loser. That movie sucked."

"Kevin, move," Ms. Ratchet said. "You're holding everyone up."

"Are you in first class?" he asked his teacher.

"No, I'm in third class and Swedish, same as you. Don't look so worried," she teased. "I'm not a Skoog."

"Whew! You could have been my mother."

In small groups, the class moved from one gallery to another, hearing stories, seeing demonstrations, viewing the exhibits, and recording facts in their "logbooks." Each gallery presented an aspect of the ship's life, from its design and construction in Belfast, Ireland, to its discovery on the ocean floor, to the recovery and conservation of hundreds of artifacts, many of which were on display.

Kevin scribbled like mad.

FACT—over 3,000,000 rivets in the hull

FACT—took 20 horses to haul each anchor to the ship (3 anchors)

FACT—4 funnels, wide enough for 2 trains to go through! Tall as an 11-story building! Heavy as 7,500 elephants!!

FACT—ship & stuff found almost 2½ miles down—sealed champagne bottle (not broken!), poker chips, kid's marble (Karl Skoog's?), jewelry, marble sink from first-class stateroom.

When he came to the display of letters, photos, and paper currency, he paused. "How come the paper stuff didn't get wrecked? Wasn't it underwater for over eighty years?"

"It's because of how it was kept," said the interpreter. "Paper items that were kept in leather wallets or leather cases were preserved."

"Amazing." Kevin noted it in his logbook. So many items, and all of them had been there—part of the ship, or part of the lives of the people who had sailed on her.

There was a model of a steam engine that actually worked, and coal samples, and stories of the men who worked in the boiler rooms—the trimmers who moved the coal from the bunkers and the firemen who shovelled it into the furnaces by hand.

Then there was the interior of the ship, with detailed re-creations of the first-, second-, and third-class cabins. Each class had its own lounge, a smoking room (for men), and a dining room. The third-class quarters weren't as luxurious as those of the other classes, but they didn't look too bad, and the people weren't crammed together like cattle.

FACT—*700 passengers in third class and 2 bathtubs!*

The tour was filled with things to do. The class could lounge on a replica *Titanic* deck chair or try on a replica life belt.

FACT—*life belts heavy, awkward, stuffed with cork, and look like vests!*

They heard about the activities on board—dining, dancing, going to concerts, swimming in the pool (for 25 cents), working out in the gymnasium on a mechanical camel or on an exercise bicycle.

The night of the disaster, first class was treated to an eleven-course dinner that included oysters, soup, salmon, chicken, steak, roast duckling, and more. How could anyone eat that much? There were two courses of dessert, one called "sweets" and the other "dessert," which was fresh fruits and cheeses.

Actors playing the role of passengers were continually strolling through the galleries. They spoke to visitors as if they, too, were passengers, asking if they'd enjoyed the band concert the night before, if they'd had a soak in the Turkish bath, if they'd eaten in the Parisian café. *"Oui!"* Kevin replied, grasping for a few French words. "I had *escargots, crème caramel* and french fries. *Très bien. Merci!"*

There was a huge cutaway model of the *Titanic*, showing the fo'c'sle deck, the well decks, the poop deck. A sailor quizzed them on nautical terms like starboard, port, crow's nest, fore, and aft.

"Why's it called a 'poop' deck?" Kevin asked. "Is it true that's where the first-class dogs went to . . . you know?"

"Nah," the sailor laughed. "A poop deck is the high deck at the back of the ship. It comes from the French word for stern."

Before long they were moving through a darkened passageway that led to a gallery called "the ice wall." The air was noticeably colder, though not as cold as it would have been on the sea that fateful night. The walls were painted black, with pinpricks of light shining through to give the illusion of stars. Towering against one wall was a dramatic replica of the iceberg. A sign next to it said *Touch.*

The interpreter invited them to go ahead. "Feel how cold it is. Can you imagine being in the North Atlantic that night, with the water temperature below freezing? Most victims died of hypothermia, and very quickly."

It was eerily silent in the last gallery. The names of 2,228 passengers and crew were projected on a wall, separated into those who survived and those who did not. The numbers were chilling: 1,517 died, 130 from first class, 166 from second class, 536 from third class, and 685 crew.

Kevin scanned the names, looking for Karl Skoog, and found him in the list of victims. He'd joked about it earlier, but seeing the boy's name up there bothered him. Especially since his friends with the first-class boarding cards had survived. "You guys bully your way onto the lifeboats?"

"*Duh,*" Brandon said. "Wouldn't you if you had the chance?"

Kevin let the question hang.

Before leaving the area, he looked to see if any Messengers had been on the *Titanic.* Nope, no one by that name. And, because the mysterious Angus Seaton was on his mind, he looked for Seaton. No one by that name, either.

Back in the classroom, after discussing the highlights of the exhibit, Ms. Ratchet brought up the moral dilemma faced by some of the passengers. The women who refused to leave their husbands. The father who handed his little sons to strangers in a lifeboat but didn't save himself. "What would you have done?" she asked.

"Not gone in the first place," said Kevin.

"Can't you take anything seriously?" Ms. Ratchet said when the laughter died down. "Forget what you know now and imagine you were there."

"Well, in that case I would've done the right thing. I would have followed the rules."

"That's a first." Brandon laughed.

"I'd follow directions and get into a lifeboat," said Natalie.

"If you were our age, like twelve or thirteen, did you count as a child?" someone asked.

"We're not children," another scoffed.

"Yeah, but if it meant life or death . . ."

"The rules said 'women and children,' and children were from one to twelve." Natalie spoke in her usual authoritative way. "Remember the story we heard about the mother and her two sons? They were fourteen and sixteen, so they were thought of as men, and they weren't allowed in the lifeboats. Their mother refused to leave without them."

"That was so sad," Hannah said. "And then she was washed overboard and ended up on an overturned lifeboat and survived. But her sons didn't."

"What if you didn't look your age, like that kid who was eleven?" Zack said. "He couldn't get on because the hat he was wearing made him look older. And what if you were tall? Too bad for you, Kev."

"I'd jump," said Kevin. "Take my chances."

"Me too," said Hannah. "The lifeboats weren't filled up, so they would've picked up anybody in the water. Except for Kevin," she added. "Who'd pick up Kevin?"

"But they didn't pick up people," Zack reminded them. "That's another moral dilemma. What would you have done if you were in a lifeboat and heard people crying for help?"

His question triggered another debate that went on until Ms. Ratchet flicked the lights to quiet things down. "Homework for Monday. Write an essay about the *Titanic* exhibit and finish off by saying what you would have done. Seriously. Got that, Kevin? Remember the new leaf."

He frowned. What was she talking about?

"Your promise, Kevin," she prompted. "Remember? Turning over—"

"Oh yeah!" He grinned.

"One more thing, everybody. Don't forget your poem assignment."

"Mine's done," Kevin said proudly. He'd done a good job too, in his opinion. Maybe he'd add some extra verses for bonus marks. Like, "Bodies, bodies, everywhere, and all the swords were red, Bodies, bodies, everywhere, 'cause everyone was dead..."

Chapter Five

Sunday, April 21, 1912

Bodies, bodies, everywhere. Bodies rolling on the blue-black sea, faceup in the drift ice, nudging and bobbing against the wreckage, against the oars and cutters of the men sent out to recover them.

Ordinary Seaman Angus Seaton, the youngest of those men, had signed on to the cable ship *Mackay-Bennett* the previous month and had boarded her that same day. His first ship! He was mighty proud to be wearing the uniform of the Commercial Cable Company, and when Sarah saw him, wouldn't she think he cut a fine figure? As an OS he'd be earning the princely wage of twenty-one dollars per month, and if he performed his duties with diligence and showed an eagerness to learn, he'd advance to an Able-Bodied Seaman in no time. And one day, God willing, he'd be a bo'sun in charge of the entire deck crew. "First things first, you daft dreamer," his bunkmate Strachan had told him, and that meant getting his sea legs. Going out on a fine day to do some fishing or set lobster pots was one thing, but plowing the icy waters of the North Atlantic for days at a time was quite another.

It was tough, dangerous work, repairing underwater telegraph cables, winching them up in stormy seas with the ice all around, but he had acquitted himself well. According to the crew, he had the makings of a first-class sailor—and not only because he'd enjoyed the daily ration of rum as much as they did.

The job finished, the *Mackay-Bennett* had returned to Halifax. Any plans for shore leave were dashed, however, when the crew was ordered to report back to the ship and prepare her for immediate departure. Not to repair another broken cable, not this time. The White Star Line had chartered the *Mackay-Bennett* to find and recover bodies. Victims of the doomed *Titanic*.

Angus and his mates had heard of the magnificent ship *Titanic*, and the news of her sinking had been met with shock and disbelief. She'd set off on her maiden voyage with such fanfare, with claims of being unsinkable. How could such a disaster have happened?

The crew had worked at a frantic pace, and, shortly after noon on April 17—two days after the *Titanic* had gone down—they were steaming full-speed out of Halifax. With a clergyman and two undertakers on board, a ton of ice in the hold, embalming fluid, and the decks stacked with coffins, the *Mackay-Bennett* already felt like a death ship.

No one had expected to find many bodies. By the time they reached the site, a whole week would have gone by. How many bodies were they likely to find? Enough to fill a hundred coffins? Never.

It was worse than anyone had expected.

Angus clutched his stomach. The sickening wave of nausea rising up in his throat—he had to control it, he couldn't be sick, he couldn't appear weak, not in front of the others. He'd taken a fair amount of ribbing his first time out, being young and inexperienced, but it was different now. They weren't repairing cables. They were handling the remains of *people*. The sight overwhelmed him. There appeared to be no end.

What had he expected? Not so many. Not the faces. Not the eyes.

Staring up at him, glazed by death, but accusing, pleading. *How did this happen? Save me...*

A prickly sensation crept across the back of his neck. When the order came, he would have to go out in a cutter. Move among the bodies. Pull them out of the water. Lay them down in the boat. Touch them. So many bodies. Two hundred coffins would not have been enough.

Chapter Six

"Stand by the boats!"

Two cutters were lowered over the side, each with a five-man crew and an assigned area to search.

Angus welcomed the strain as he pulled on the oars. The ache in his muscles would go away soon enough, unlike the ache in a deeper part of himself. That, he feared, could take a long time to heal.

The bodies floated high in the water, the life belts holding them up in spite of the sodden clothing. Nudging and bobbing against each other, bumping against the cutters and oars, rising and falling in the heavy swell, in and out of the drifting ice. A macabre dance played out to the rhythm of wind and waves.

"Hold steady!" Strachan said. "We're bringing one in."

Angus struggled to keep the cutter steady as Strachan stood up with the pike and hooked it around the life belt of a ten- to twelve-year-old boy. Two sailors hauled his body on board.

"Still in knickers, poor little blighter," Strachan said. "May he rest in peace."

Angus wanted to weep. He tried not to think of the excitement that boy must have felt on boarding the biggest, most luxurious ship ever built. Stepping up the gangway in his best clothes—the same as now, most likely—his black boots polished, stockings pulled up just so, his gray knickers... the lad not quite old enough to wear long trousers. He'd never know that proud moment in a boy's life.

And at the end, was the boy too late to get on a lifeboat? Angus pushed the thought away. He tried not to think of the boy's terror. He tried, willed himself, not to think. Willed himself to put aside any thoughts of the victims' lives and to concentrate on doing his job.

They had picked up one female body and were about to retrieve another when a small form, floating without a life belt, came up alongside the cutter. Angus sucked in a breath, felt his eyes well up. This little one, a fair-haired child no more than two years old—it was hard to tell with toddlers—this little one could be his undoing.

Strachan lifted the child out of the water and gently laid him down. Someone who loved him had dressed him for the cold. A little gray coat with fur on the collar and cuffs, a brown serge frock underneath. Brown shoes and stockings.

A deep and respectful stillness fell over the men. In a voice heavy with emotion, Strachan said, "If no one claims his body, I'll pay for his funeral myself."

"We'll all pay a share," said Reilly.

Angus could no longer hold back the tears. The thought of the little lad crying for his mother... "Oh, God," he said, wiping his eyes. "Sorry, mates."

"No need," Strachan said. "We're all taking it hard."

The others nodded, visibly shaken.

It didn't take long for Angus to become familiar with the recovery system. The captain and officers kept watch on the bridge and fo'c'sle and, whenever they spotted wreckage and bodies, they signaled the location with flags and whistles. The men in the cutters then went to the area, picked up the bodies a few at a time, and took them to the ship.

One by one the bodies were lifted over the ship's rail and onto the deck, each numbered in the order it came up to the rail. The numbers were recorded in the ship's log and stenciled onto a piece of canvas tied to each body. A canvas bag for any personal effects was given the same number. No chance, then, of the silver watch found on Body No. 39 being put into the bag containing the medallion marked *B.V.M.* found on Body No. 12. Or the loaded revolver found on Body No. 15 ending up with the Sailors' and Firemen's Union badge belonging to Body No. 30. The system, as Angus saw it, was foolproof.

By the time the two cutters were hoisted up, the men had been working for ten hours and had brought in fifty-one bodies.

Angus swallowed hard. Would he ever get used to it? A few of the bodies they'd found had smashed-up faces, broken limbs, or crushed skulls, evidence of having been shattered by the cables, rigging, davits, and funnels that must have toppled over and broken apart as the ship was going down. Most of the bodies looked as though they were asleep, the faces calm and peaceful.

"Didn't have a chance, not in this water," Strachan said. "They would have died quick and painless, I should think."

Angus agreed. Relatively painless, once the first icy bite froze all sense of feeling. He knew the numbing effect of the North Atlantic.

Fifty-one bodies...Angus dreaded to think what the next day would bring.

Dinner that night was a solemn affair. No one felt like talking or bantering. They were thankful when the Chief Steward passed around the customary pail of English rum, and, when they learned that the captain had ordered double rations for the duration of the voyage, they sent up a rousing cheer. The heartiness didn't last. The rum did little to raise their spirits.

At sunset the tolling of the ship's bell summoned all hands to the fo'c'sle. Some of the bodies, even though they'd been identified through personal effects, were too badly injured to be embalmed. Others had no personal effects to help with identification.

It was the first time Angus had attended a sea burial. He stood with his shipmates on the rolling deck, their heads bowed, their hats in their hands. Each time a body was brought to the rail, Canon Hind, the clergyman, intoned the words of the service. "I am the resurrection and the life, saith the Lord. . . . We therefore commit his body to the deep."

There was an interval of silence as the body, weighted and wrapped in canvas, slid off the rail. A silence broken by a splash as it hit the water. Its number recorded in the log with the words *Buried at sea.*

For almost an hour the crew stood in the cold, frozen in an eerie tableau, bearing witness to the twenty-four bodies committed to the deep.

After the service Angus accompanied his mates to the crew's General Room. He'd been inclined to retreat to his quarters but, knowing he'd be unable to sleep, he'd changed his mind. Better to work on his wreck-wood project than lie in the dark, dwelling on the day, worrying about the next one, getting depressed about it all.

He'd done some whittling when he was a kid, but the wood had been nothing special, not like the wreck wood he and the others had picked up while out in the cutters. Sections of painted wood, intricately carved moldings, bits of carved oak that might have been part of the ship's grand staircase. Some of the crew had picked up whole items. A cutting board, a rolling pin, a drawer from what might have been a dresser in a first-class stateroom.

Several men, experienced hands by the look of it, already had a project going. One sailor was making a chessboard, another a paperweight; someone else was carving a small dory.

"Any ideas, Strachan?" Angus was at a loss.

Strachan glanced up from the cribbage board he was making. "Sharpen your knife, for a start. That thing you're using is for butter."

Angus cracked a grin. "Seriously, Strachan. You're the expert."

"Not me. Howell's the expert around here. He'll have a whole chess set by the time we're through. Show him, Howell."

A king and a queen, beautifully made. "I'm carving a set for my son," Howell said. "Here's a bit of advice, Seaton. Look at all the wood before you start. See how the pieces might fit together. Colors, textures, the grain, that sort of thing. Wreck wood like this, you'll never see the likes again. They spared no expense building that ship. Where are you ever going to find pieces of teak and mahogany for the taking?"

"Hadn't thought of it like that," said Angus.

"The way I see it, you got a responsibility," the older man went on. "Sailors keep something from a shipwreck as a souvenir—always have done, always will—and they pass it on. So a bit of history is kept in the family. And if it's something from a famous ship, like the *Titanic*, it's a treasure. See what I'm saying?"

"Hadn't thought of that, either," Angus said.

"When're you going to start thinking? Soon, I hope, before you cut off a thumb with that knife you're twiddling."

The men joined in the ribbing at Angus's expense. He welcomed it, the way it lightened the mood.

Chapter Seven

"Thank God we're done," Angus said as the cutter was hoisted for the night.

"Amen to that," said Strachan. "And thank God we had a calm sea."

The day had been exhausting. Bodies were showing up in ever-growing numbers but, thanks to the calm sea, they'd been able to carry up to nine at a time, rather than five or six, without fear of being swamped.

It was the worst day yet in recovering bodies. All told, the cutters had brought in a hundred twenty-eight.

Many of the bodies had been wearing uniforms, a clue that marked them as crewmen. Stokers, trimmers, seamen, stewards. Some must have escaped the sinking ship only to die in the frigid water. Others, marked by burns and broken limbs, must have been killed on board and their bodies swept off the decks by the sea.

Angus had lost count of the number of trips they'd made to the ship. Ten? Twelve? Back and forth to the ship, pulling hard at the oars or taking his turn at the tiller, breath steaming into icy clouds, the grim task never easing up. More bodies to be numbered and recorded, more personal effects to be bagged and tagged. He longed to be back in port, to tear off his clothing, peel away his skin, throw himself into something that didn't scream of death.

The next day the weather turned brutal. Heavy swells, a fierce sea, a fog so dense the officers spotting from the bridge couldn't see the ship's length, let alone a body. And cold! Ten minutes on deck, and a man's hair and eyebrows were frosted with ice.

There was no point taking out the cutters and running the risk of being swamped, so Angus was assigned to assist in the documenting of bodies and personal effects. It was a daunting task and, with two hundred five bodies recovered so far, not close to being done. Every article of clothing had to be removed and searched. Pockets turned inside out and linings examined in case of hidden treasures, like the diamonds that had rolled out of a fellow's coat lining the previous day. Not just two or three diamonds, but seventeen.

The small canvas bags, numbered to match the identification numbers of the bodies, held all manner of jewelry, watches, coins, and the like, personal items that would go to relatives once the body was claimed. If a body could not be identified, anything that could help give it a name was noted. A chemise marked *B.H.* in red. A bead necklace. A sum of 150 Finnish marks sewed inside clothing. A steward's uniform with the White Star Line badge. Boots, size 8. A blue tattoo on a man's right arm, depicting an angel of love. The smallest detail could connect an unidentified body to a loved one.

"This one meant to survive, didn't he?" Angus said. He and Strachan were recording the articles of clothing they'd removed from a man's body. "Pajamas, three shirts, two pairs of pants, two vests, two jackets, and an overcoat. Must have put on every bit of clothing he had with him."

Strachan nodded. "He was hoping to survive the cold, anyhow. Couldn't have been in a hurry, either, taking time to put all that on."

"Even put meat and biscuits in his pockets," said Angus. "Did he have a child with him, do you think? Maybe that's who the food was for. What do you think?"

"I *don't* think," Strachan said. "I'd advise you to do the same. Dwelling on it the way you do, it could drive you mad."

"I've been trying not to, but I can't help wondering. You know, where they were from and where they were going, what their lives were like." Except for the first-class passengers, and there was no mystery about their lives. The items Angus had recorded from Body No. 124 had been enough of a clue: belt with gold buckle, gold watch, gold cufflinks with diamonds, a diamond ring with three stones, a gold pencil and over two thousand dollars in cash. The body was identified as John Jacob Astor, said to be the wealthiest man in the world. Still, there he was, as dead as the others. His relatives would learn his fate before the *Mackay-Bennett* even returned to Halifax, for each night the captain wired the names of the identified bodies to the White Star Line, which notified the next of kin.

At least J. J. Astor had the luxury of a coffin. He wasn't covered up by a tarp, the way Body No. 125 was about to be.

Body No. 125, about seventeen, wearing a steward's uniform over white and green striped pajamas, black button boots, a gold wedding ring.

Who was the seventeen-year-old steward? Angus wondered. Same age as himself, and already married. He must have been asleep when the ship hit the iceberg. Leaped out of bed, threw on his uniform...

Angus sighed heavily. Told himself for the umpteenth time to stop thinking, and went back to the job at hand.

After the noon meal the tolling of the ship's bells summoned all hands for another sea burial. They hadn't had any burials the day before, as they'd run out of canvas to wrap the bodies. But that same night they'd met up with a passing ship and replenished their supply.

For the third time in four days, Angus stood watch as one canvas-shrouded body after another slid over the rail and into the sea, Canon Hind intoning the now-familiar words.

I commit your body to the deep.

Silence.

A splash.

I commit your body to the deep.

Silence.

A splash.

I commit your body . . .

Seventy-seven times.

At the end of the service, when the sailors had been dismissed and were going their various ways, it struck Angus more keenly than ever how much the ship had become a morgue. Recovering the bodies was a painful task, but you could at least set your mind on the sea and the physical struggle. Working on board, surrounded by bodies and personal effects and trying to make sense of something that had no sense, well, that was another thing altogether. There was no escape. It was almost impossible to move about the ship, with the poop deck stacked high with coffins, the cable wells lined with bodies, the forward hold filled with bodies piled one on top of the other. Death was everywhere.

"Are you working on your box tonight?" Strachan said as they were nearing the General Room. "It's looking grand."

Angus shook his head. "I don't trust myself with a knife in my hand. The mood I'm in, you might have my body to tag tomorrow."

"Jaysus, don't talk like that. Don't even think it."

Angus managed a small smile and retreated to his quarters.

He lay on his bunk, hoping to catch a few hours' sleep before his night watch. He hadn't meant what he'd said to Strachan. He'd never feel *that* low, not with Sarah waiting for him at home and, God willing, a wedding sometime soon. Not for a while, really, but come his first paycheck, he could buy her an engagement ring. He brightened at the thought. A ring with a small diamond and their initials engraved inside the band . . .

He stopped short, realizing that he was picturing a ring he'd removed from a finger earlier that day and bagged. A shiver ran through him. The thought of Sarah, picked up from the water by a stranger, her ring ending up in a canvas bag . . . it was impossible to imagine. He vowed he would never, ever, take her to sea.

Chapter Eight

Late afternoon, and the light was beginning to fade. Another hard and exhausting day for Angus and the crew in the cutter, but it was nearing the end. With any luck, the bodies they were approaching would be the last.

Five men clinging together in a group. Angus, unable to stop his mind from wandering, wondered how they'd come to be together. Friends, hanging on till the end? Strangers, not wanting to die without the closeness of another? Did they think that a huddle would help them to survive by keeping them warm? Tears stung his eyes. It wasn't good to think or imagine what might have been going through their minds at the end. Not right at the end, no, because the shock of the cold would have killed any thought, wouldn't it? But their thoughts before the end, when they knew what was about to happen, when there was no hope of rescue and the lifeboats were gone—

"Seaton! To starboard!"

Angus's head snapped up. He hadn't been paying attention. What was he thinking, dozing off while the others were struggling?

There was a body, riding the crest of an oncoming wave, not an arm's length from the side of the boat. As the others were occupied on the port side, hauling in the bodies of the five men, it was up to Angus to bring this one in. It almost rolled into his arms, it was so close, and by God, it was the body of a girl.

The shock made his knees buckle. They'd recovered few female bodies, and this one was so young, no more than sixteen or seventeen by his reckoning. He leaned out, took hold of her life belt, and hauled her up to the gunnel. How was it she hadn't gotten into a lifeboat? Had she jumped from the rail or been swept off the deck? Had she left anyone behind? Parents, a brother or sister . . .

There he was, thinking again.

She had a lovely face. Smooth, unblemished like Sarah's, and the same dark hair. Her mouth, partly open—had she been calling out to someone at the end? Her deep-set eyes, the darkest blue he'd ever seen, wide open— had she been searching for someone, desperate to see that someone, even at the moment of death? Angus blinked hard and looked away.

The cutter gave a sudden lurch. Fearful that the girl's body would slide back into the sea, Angus made a frantic effort to drag it over the gunnel. He had to be quick, as the others were having a rough time with the men's bodies and, with no one at the tiller and the wind picking up and the sun going down, the work was becoming more dangerous.

Another lurch, and the cutter was rolling into a trough and then, blast it, something fell out from within the girl's clothing. Angus lunged, the sudden action causing him to fall backward and the men to curse, but he caught it, dropped it into his pocket, and turned his attention to the body teetering on the gunnel. Grabbed hold and, with all the force he could muster, pulled it down and into the cutter. Then back to the tiller as the cutter rode to the crest of another wave.

Body No. 61. Female, light hair, estimated age of thirty, red cardigan—

That wasn't right. The girl wasn't Body No. 61. *That* female was brought in the second day. Or was it the third day?

—black woollen shawl, blue tattoo on upper arm, black moustache, only four upper teeth, large wart on index finger—

"No!" Angus cried out. The sound jolted him from sleep. The bodies had to stop. They had to stay out of his head. He was confusing them, turning them into a muddle of bits and pieces put into the wrong bags—it had to stop. He had to sleep. He was on watch in a few hours, and if he didn't get some sleep... He'd let the crew down once by not paying attention; he couldn't let it happen again.

He fell back into his bunk and closed his eyes, praying, praying for sleep.

Two hours later he was awakened by the watch bell. He was grateful for it, too, as he'd been in the middle of another disturbing dream. Canvas bags stuffed with fish and bones and body parts and a girl's face chiselled out of ice and the ice beginning to melt.

Slipping on his clothes, Angus realized that the face in his dream was that of the girl he'd recovered the day before. They'd be documenting her body today, provided that they'd caught up on the backlog. Someone would note the details—female, about seventeen, black hair, long black overcoat....

He was buttoning his coat when it struck him. The object he'd saved from falling into the sea—he hadn't turned it in. It was still in his pocket. A small leather purse with something inside.

Curious though he was, it was not up to him to open the purse, not until it had been recorded, bagged, and tagged to match the number on the body. But what was the number?

He smacked his forehead with the heel of his hand, cursing under his breath. How could he have been so careless? To forget to hand in the one item that could help identify the girl? After recording such items himself, and knowing their importance? Unforgiveable. And now he couldn't remember the number! If he could remember *when* her body came over the rail, if it was before or after the five male bodies—no, wait. He calmed himself. They'd recovered such a small number of female bodies, hers would be easy to find. So long as it wasn't buried in one of the piles.

Almost four o'clock. He was due to report to the repair room where the personal effects were being bagged. If her body happened to be one of the ones being documented, he could slip the purse in without anyone being the wiser. The likelihood of that happening...no, he couldn't take the chance. Besides, it wasn't the right thing to do.

The right thing to do was to report to the duty officer and turn in the purse. That was a worry. Would he be charged for negligence, or accused of stealing from the dead? In his defense he could say that he'd put it in his pocket and forgotten, what with the confusion at the time, his pulling in the body and manning the tiller and trying to steady the cutter while the other men were hauling in five bodies, not to mention the fading light and a rough sea...no, on second thought, there was no need to make excuses. He'd simply forgotten. He'd hand over the purse, apologize, and take the consequences.

He was on his way to report when he was stopped by a commotion in the passageway. An oiler, clearly in a state of panic, was trying to explain something to an officer.

"It almost knocks me over!" the poor man was stammering. "The second engineer gives me a message to take to the watch officer and I go out of the engine room to do just that and the body's in the passageway. Moving up and down in the passageway. I'm telling you, sir, it was alive—"

"Calm down, man," the officer said. "Seaton, report to the engineer and find out what's going on."

Angus nodded. A body, alive? Was it possible that someone had survived after all? What if the crew had made the wrong assumption? If they had checked for vital signs..."Oh, for God's sake, Angus!" he muttered. "Get ahold of yourself. You're as bad as the oiler."

He reported to the engineer, and was ordered to assist the deck crew in securing the bodies in the passageway.

It was easy to see what had happened. There was such a pile of bodies, the pitching of the ship had caused one of them to become dislodged. It had slid off the pile and was rolling in front of the engine-room door at the very moment when the oiler had stepped out.

"I would have been in a panic, too," Angus said to his fellow sailors. "Surrounded by dead, day and night, at work, at rest, how could you help it?" They had a few laughs at the oiler's expense—poor fellow would never live it down—and were surprised to find that they could laugh at such a time. It was a welcome change.

It wasn't until much later in the day that Angus remembered what he'd been meaning to do. The incident with the oiler had been the start of one thing after another, and the fact was he'd forgotten, again, to hand in the purse.

Should he do it now? No, one more day wouldn't make a difference at this point. Besides, he was in the middle of working on his wreck-wood box. He had come up with a new idea and was pleased at how well it was turning out. Howell, whose carvings Angus so much admired, was calling his box "a work of art."

And why not? Angus was making it as a gift for Sarah. When the time came, there'd be a little diamond ring hidden inside.

Chapter Nine

The mission was over for the *Mackay-Bennett* and her crew. After another wrenching day, they received word that the cable ship *Minia* was coming to relieve them. Five days later, after having been out for a total of thirteen days, the *Mackay-Bennett* was slowly steaming into Halifax. A death ship.

She came up the harbor in the early morning, on water as still as a mirror, her flag at half-mast, her decks stacked high with unshrouded bodies and coffins, the crew at the rails, bare-headed and solemn.

The tolling of church bells marked their passage. Flags throughout the city and across the Narrows in Dartmouth hung at half-mast, not a single breeze to stir them. Windows of homes and shops were draped in black. Silent crowds stood vigil along the waterfront, on the slopes of Citadel Hill, on rooftops, and in the area around the Dockyard. All stood silent, their heads bare. A steady stream of hearses, carriages, and motor vehicles could be seen passing through the Dockyard gates.

At nine thirty the *Mackay-Bennett* was alongside the Flagship Pier. The crew carried out the business of docking at an unhurried pace, and officers gave orders in hushed voices. Church bells continued to toll.

Bodies that had not been placed in coffins were the first to be removed from the ship. The crew laid the bodies on stretchers, one by one, then carried them down the gangway and onto the waiting wagons.

Angus followed the bodies in his mind as the wagons took them away. Their next stop would be a makeshift morgue at the edge of town. They'd lie there waiting for someone to identify or claim them. Some would be taken home to be buried, if their next of kin could afford it. Others, with or without a name, claimed or unclaimed, would be buried in Halifax.

The last bodies to be removed were first-class passengers, each one identified, embalmed, and placed in a coffin. Cranes picked them up, one by one, and lowered them onto the wharf. Hearses and undertakers' wagons took them away.

Close to a hundred mourners waited at the gate. Some of the mourners notified by the White Star Line had traveled to Halifax from places in the United States. Some were *Titanic* survivors who had traveled from New York after arriving there on board the rescue ship *Carpathia*.

Other mourners were family members who had not received word. They waited with anxious dread, praying that one of the unidentified bodies might be that of their loved one.

Angus wondered if "his" girl's family would be among them. He hadn't seen a detailed description of her clothing or a list of items found on her person. A locket or letter found in an inside pocket or sewn into a lining—there could be any number of things he hadn't noticed when he'd recovered her body. They wouldn't have to have the purse he'd found.

He groaned, shaken by the familiar sinking in the pit of his stomach. He'd meant to turn in the purse, but he'd been distracted. Then he'd forgotten. Then, on remembering, he was afraid it was too late. An apology was not good enough now. He would most certainly be punished.

He'd put the purse in his sea chest without opening it, deciding it was better not to know. The purse itself was nothing special. He should have let it fall into the sea when he had the chance. He could still do that—pretend he'd never had it—but he felt strangely compelled to keep it. For the same reason, he supposed, as he was keeping the pieces of wreck wood.

There'd been so many bodies. Three hundred six was the last number they'd recorded. One hundred sixteen buried at sea, one hundred ninety brought to shore. The *Minia* would no doubt bring in more.

The child they'd found on the first day, his little body tagged as Body No. 4... how long ago that seemed. The entire crew had agreed to pay for his casket and funeral if nobody claimed the body. After that, God willing, the ordeal would be over.

After three and a half hours, the last coffin was removed.

Sunlight glinted off the water, a hopeful sign. The company that owned the *Mackay-Bennett* had wired Captain Larnder the night before, saying that the officers and men would receive double pay for the time they'd been engaged, in appreciation of their efficient and humanitarian work. It was welcome news, though no one was in a mood to celebrate.

The crew also received new orders. The cable they'd repaired the previous month had been broken again, possibly by the same iceberg, and they were to report for regular duty in two days' time.

"Thank God." Exhausted though he was, Angus sighed with relief. Some time with Sarah and his parents, then a tough slog on the North Atlantic to clear his mind of death and sorrow. The very thing he needed.

Chapter Ten

Kevin was out of the car before his dad had even set the emergency brake. "Couldn't you have rented a bigger car, Dad? My legs are like pretzels." He took a minute to stretch out the kinks, glad of his father's decision to park at the bottom of the wooded driveway so they could "get the feel of the place" and approach the house on foot. Without waiting for the others, Kevin took off at a run. Shearwater Point! The mystery house! Finally, they'd arrived.

They'd left Halifax at seven that morning. Since then they'd been in and out of the car, sightseeing along Nova Scotia's "Lighthouse Route" where, according to the tourist brochures, "the past is a part of everyday life." They'd stopped at fishing villages like Peggy's Cove and old towns like Lunenburg, listened to stories about shipwrecks, privateers, and the *Bluenose* (the tall ship that appeared on the Canadian dime), and taken pictures of lobster traps, lighthouses, and a million other things, including goofy ones of each other.

Kevin had enjoyed the journey and had done as much "Wow-ing" as his parents and Courtney. But by midafternoon he'd had enough. If he heard one more historical fact or had to stop at one more historical whatever, he was going to go AWOL.

Even their time in Halifax had been taken up with history. Stunning history, like in the Maritime Museum of the Atlantic, where they had exhibits on two disasters—the 1917 Halifax Explosion that killed close to 2,000 people, and the sinking of the *Titanic*. Kevin hadn't known that the victims' bodies had been brought to Halifax, and that many of them had been buried in a local cemetery. He had stayed on by himself to take in more of the *Titanic* exhibit while the rest of the family went off for coffee. He could have spent hours in that museum alone.

His father had returned from his Nova Scotia trip in May, totally sold on the property at Shearwater Point. Turned out that he hadn't inherited the property *directly* from Angus Seaton—he'd died over thirty years ago—but from his son, Myles Seaton. Myles had died in February 2010 and had left the property to James Messenger, according to provisions laid out in Angus Seaton's will.

That's what Kevin remembered, anyway. The whole business was complicated and confusing and weird. His father must have thought the same thing, because he'd told Kevin and his mum to stop searching for answers, at least until the summer when they were at the place and settled in. That's when he planned to figure things out. When you see it, he'd assured them, you'll love it so much you won't care about the whos and the whys, you'll only be thinking, Lucky us.

He'd been big on telling everyone about the place, describing various features as the best this, the greatest that, the most fantastic something else. But showing it, as in sending some photos of the house instead of just the beach and the view? "You'll have to trust me," he'd said. He wanted it to be a surprise.

Kevin had been sold on the beach from the outset and couldn't wait to go in for a swim. But first, the big question. What would the house be like? As he came round a curve in the driveway he had his answer: an old, two-story house practically strangled by weeds and bushes in a seriously overgrown yard. As a setting for a horror movie, it was perfect. Shuttered windows, wooden shingles, accessible by a driveway winding through dark, scrubby trees. He pictured the film credits: Kevin Messenger, star of *The Edge of Gloom*. Or *Whose Insane Idea Was It?*

"Welcome to Shearwater Point, everybody," his father said. "Isn't it something?"

Kevin and Courtney exchanged glances. "Did you really have this place checked out, Dad?" Courtney asked. "Looks like it might be infested."

"Don't be silly!" he laughed. "The backyard hasn't been cleared yet, that's all. Look, I told you it wasn't a mansion. Come on, let's join your mum out front."

Kevin stayed put. "You called it interesting. Full of character. You said it had a 'weathered charm.'"

"It does! Sure, it needs some work, but it's got good bones. You haven't seen the front yet, and you haven't been inside. And wait till you see the beach. It's better than in the pictures. Laura, honey!" he called out. "How do you like the verandah? C'mon, Kev. This is an adventure!"

Kevin grimaced. Jim Messenger, supporting actor in *The Edge of Gloom*, irritatingly cheerful. An adventure—was Dad serious? It looked like work, a DIY project for the summer.

He was about to ask how long they had to stay when his dad slapped an arm around his shoulders and said, "Don't be negative."

"What? I didn't say anything!"

"Your face says it all. Remember, we're in this together." He tightened his grip on Kevin's shoulder. "Got it?"

Kevin pulled away and trudged around to the front, expecting the worst. He stopped short. "Not bad!" The words came out involuntarily. With two large gables on the roof, a wide verandah running across its length, and a sandy beach a few yards from the door, the house looked a thousand times more inviting from this angle.

His parents were standing at the front door. "You kids got your cameras ready? Here goes!" His dad unlocked the door and, to Kevin's embarrassment—thank God there was no one around—he swooped his wife into his arms and carried her across the threshold.

"Awesome picture, guys!" Courtney laughed. "Take one of Kevin carrying me."

"Get real," Kevin snorted, and ventured inside.

"This looks promising," his mother was saying. "The fireplace, furniture, high ceiling—so much space."

Kevin was at a loss. The room had a musty smell from being closed up for who knew how long, but what if it was mold? Black mold growing rampant in the walls and ceilings, attacking him with deadly toxins or patho-something bacteria or whatever. He kept the thought to himself.

"Right, then, team. Down to business." His father clapped his hands for attention. "First thing we have to do is—"

"Go swimming!" Kevin said.

His father scowled. "Not so fast. We need your help. First thing is to open the shutters and windows, top and bottom, let in the light and give the place a good airing out. It'll make the world of difference. By the time that's done and we've got the car unloaded and everything unpacked, it'll be happy hour, swimming time, whatever you like. What do you say? Aren't you glad we left early this morning? Let's go, team!"

An hour or so later, things were looking better. Kevin was quick to claim one of the two upstairs bedrooms, even though he kept bashing his head on the sloping ceiling. He liked the iron bed and the wooden trunk with rope handles that served as a bedside table. His mother called it a sea chest, which made them think that Angus Seaton might have been a sailor.

Kevin opened it eagerly, hoping to find some more clues about Angus Seaton. But no, the chest was empty.

The house was equally empty in terms of clues, though it was full of surprises. Mostly stuff that Kevin's father had bought on his earlier trip, like new mattresses, bed linen, towels, dishes, and kitchen appliances. With the help of the property manager, he'd even arranged to have the entire place repainted and the bathroom renovated before the family arrived.

The property manager had taken care of other necessities, too, like food. He'd been in the day before and stocked the fridge with milk, juice, beer and soft drinks, bread, butter, cheese, and fruit.

The unpacking done, everyone grabbed a cold drink and retreated to the verandah.

"This is the life," Kevin's father said, sinking into one of the deck chairs.

"Imagine. Drinks and snacks on our verandah, taking in the view of our own private beach on the Atlantic Ocean . . . can you believe it? Talk about a windfall."

"I personally *don't* believe it," Kevin said. "Look. It's not something you won in a raffle, Dad. It was left to you for a reason. Didn't the lawyer or the property manager guy tell you anything about Angus Seaton?"

"Look, I'll go over it again," his dad said. "When Myles Seaton was having his will drawn up, he gave his lawyer a copy of Angus Seaton's will and told him he wanted to honor his father's wishes concerning the property at Shearwater Point. According to the lawyer, Myles didn't want the property, he had no children to think of, and he respected his father's reasons for the legacy."

Kevin frowned. "So why didn't he put them in the will?"

"God, Kevin! I don't know. And the lawyer didn't know. But he assured me it's perfectly legal. People grant bequests all the time without spelling out the reasons."

"You've got to be curious, though. I say we find out."

"Of course I'm curious," his dad said. "But we can't tackle everything at once. We spend a couple of days settling in, then we start to ask questions. We can use the laptop as soon as the Internet's hooked up. Meanwhile, there's a library in the village. We can start there. For now, let's sit back and enjoy our good fortune."

"There's got to be a catch," said Kevin.

Courtney gave him a playful punch in the arm. "Lighten up. You're such a pessimist. Dad's right. Just accept the fact that good things can happen."

"Yeah, but—no offense, Dad—why would *this* particular good thing happen to *you?*" He jumped aside as his father made to swat him, and, laughing, ran down to the beach for his long-awaited swim.

Chapter Eleven

The next morning Kevin woke up at a ridiculous hour. With daylight coming in and the crash of breaking waves—so close you'd think the beach was in the next room—there was no hope of getting back to sleep, so he got up and threw on some clothes. A visit to the kitchen for a granola bar and a juice box, and he was off to explore.

A clue about Angus Seaton could turn up anywhere. So the first thing to do was make a thorough inspection of the property. Then he'd go for a swim—provided the tide had come in a ways—and send a message to Zack. Something like *2 swims in 2 days. Water like ice. How's that for dedication?*

He made his way to the shed that he could see from his bedroom window. It had the same wooden shingles and shutters as the house, and double doors at the front secured by a tough-looking padlock. He hoped to find a crack or an opening so he could look in, but it was sealed up tight. It seemed logical that there'd be a boat inside, but if there wasn't, what a perfect place to keep one. You could pull it out, slide it down the slope to the water, and go anywhere.

He left the boat shed and climbed up the spruce-covered hill that rose from the southern end of the beach, up and over the crest, and down to the granite boulders that formed the tip of Shearwater Point.

Finally the map he'd seen of the area made sense. To the left was Plover Beach, a half-mile-long stretch of sand and dunes that curved around a bay to the village of Ragged Harbour. To the right was another curved bay, ending in a causeway and a breakwater lined with small wooden buildings—sheds, fish houses, cabins. There was a small island off the breakwater that he'd be able to walk to when the tide was out, the way it was now.

On the far side of the breakwater were a couple of fishing boats and a pier. Not much activity, though some parked vehicles indicated that there could be people sleeping in the cabins. More likely they'd gone out fishing. The water was amazingly clear. He hadn't noticed on his swim the day before—hadn't noticed anything other than the insane temperature of the water—but now, looking down from his position high up on the rocks, he could see the bottom, could practically count the stones, it was so clear. It would be a great spot for diving.

He drained the last of his juice and started back, wondering what to do next. The village, he decided. He could go to the library before the others got around to it, ask about Angus Seaton, send a message to Zack. He'd stop at the house, get something more to eat, and find a beach towel. He'd have a swim at Plover Beach on the way back from the village, and another swim at his own beach. He'd be used to the cold water in no time.

Dad was right. Why not relax and enjoy their good fortune? No bumming a ride or waiting for a bus to get to a beach, like he had to do at home. Hey, he could go swimming three times a day if he wanted to. How stunning was that? He went into the house humming.

"Morning, Kevin!" His mother greeted him from the kitchen. "Sounds like you're in a good mood. Sit down, have some breakfast. We've been waiting for you."

"You shouldn't have," he said, glancing sidewise at his dad to see if he'd picked up on the sarcasm. Don't be negative, he reminded himself, but cripes, he'd never get away now.

He sat down and poured a bowl of cereal. "Dad, you know that shed—not the tool shed, the other one? Can I have the key? I think it's a boat shed. Mum, is there any toast?"

"Sorry," she said. "Someone forgot to buy a toaster."

"And a coffee maker." Courtney stuck out her chin and scowled at the jar of instant. "And don't forget the Internet connection."

"Don't worry, folks," their father said. "It's all on the list. Can't cover everything at once."

"Dad, what about the key? There must be a boat in there."

"Later, Kevin. There's plenty of time. Now, everybody listen up. Last night your mum and I made a to-do list and a schedule."

"A schedule? We're on vacation!" Kevin's jaw dropped. "Jeez, Dad, I've got my own things to do. Like swimming, remember? You said I could swim every day. And what about the boat shed? Can't we at least have a look? You never said anything about a schedule."

"Attitude, son. I know we're on vacation, but there are certain things that have to be done, and the sooner we get them done the more time we'll have to enjoy ourselves. You'll have plenty of time for swimming and looking in the boat shed. And here's an incentive for you: anything you find in the basement, you can keep."

"Who said I was doing the basement?"

"I thought you'd prefer it. Downstairs, away from the cheerfuls."

"That's not fair. Why not Courtney? She doesn't look so cheerful. Why don't you pick on her for a change?"

"Don't start—"

"Chill, Dad." Courtney cut him off before he got too worked up. "I'll do the basement. It'll be way cooler down there. Okay, Kev?"

"Forget it." Kevin got up in a huff. It'd be nice to have a choice for once, but to be *assigned* the basement, with no consideration or consultation? Jeez. So much for being "in this together." Why didn't his dad do the basement? Had he seen what a mess it was and thought, Good place for Kevin? Keep him out of the way for a while?

He slammed the wall with his fist to make a point, and opened the basement door. Just when he was starting to like the place, and thinking about a boat—ha! Like he'd have a say in that.

He switched on the light. "Kevin Messenger, star of *Nothing*," he muttered. "Descends into the gloom, stumbles onto a heap of moldy bones and a dismembered corpse—whoa!"

Even in the dim light he could see that they'd need a truck to clear out the stuff. At least it was clean stuff, and there was no sign of body parts. No sign of anything but newspapers. Towers of newspapers, with a maze of narrow aisles separating one tower from the other. Towers so high he'd need a ladder to reach the top. So he could keep whatever he liked, huh? Big wow.

There was room to walk around, but only if he kept his elbows in. Some of the towers looked way tippy. The slightest nudge could knock over a stack, and the domino effect would take care of the rest. Kevin Messenger, buried alive in comic strips, old news, and obituaries.

The walls were covered with heavy black paper that had come loose in places, showing the building studs underneath. Nothing of interest there, but the far wall, the one that couldn't be seen from the stairs, that was something else. A small section was covered with boards. A mishmash of boards, all shapes and sizes, hammered on top of each other in a crisscross pattern.

Well. If someone had wanted to hammer a bucket of nails into every board that washed up on the beach, he must have had a reason. Had he hidden something behind the boards?

"Only one way to find out," Kevin said. The others had called down that they were going to Shelburne for supplies. Plenty of time for a little demolition...

It wasn't long before Kevin realized that the task he'd given himself was tougher than the one his dad had given him. "Smart move, Messenger," he grunted, yanking off another board. Should have left it till later and gotten Dad to help. A joint project, uncovering a mystery together—on second thought, it was probably better this way. When they came back and discovered what he'd found—hey, it could be a Big Clue about Angus Seaton.

Good thing the others had gone out. They would've been snooping around in no time, the racket he was making. Groaning, grunting, babbling, cursing, prying away a board only to find another, tossing boards and nails to the floor, but at least he was making progress.

What had Angus Seaton been thinking? Assuming that he was the one responsible. Fifty-plus nails in every board—must have been a heck of a sale. Had he planned to cover the whole basement that way, to keep the damp from wrecking the newspapers? Some carpenter. Maybe drywall was too expensive. Maybe it hadn't been invented. Maybe it had nothing to do with the basement. Maybe the guy went berserk for some reason and attacked a pile of boards. Better than attacking a person. Or did the boards come after he'd attacked a person?

Kevin laughed out loud. "No way I'm going to find a skeleton in there," he said. "But man, there better be something after all this work."

Time for a breather. He took off his T-shirt and used it to wipe his forehead. The boards he'd dropped to the floor were becoming a hazard, the way the rusty nails were sticking up. He kicked them aside, careful not to disturb the newspaper towers, and went back to work. A couple of hours later he was almost done. A few more boards, a sheet of plywood, some more black paper by the looks of it, and he'd uncover the hidden—something. Then he'd go for a swim. Why not? Nobody said he had to keep working while the others were joy-riding around the countryside, stopping for ice cream or lobster rolls or whatever. Yeah, a swim, and a walk to the village, just like he'd planned. Unless he released a vampire or something out of the living dead. "Better be a good reason, Angus Seaton," he muttered, "or I'll take this crowbar and smash down the wall. Surprise, Dad! The house has collapsed. Okay...here goes—" The last nail came out with a satisfying screech.

And *voilà!*

A cubbyhole? Kevin flung down the crowbar in disgust. The big secret was nothing more than a small cupboard with empty shelves. Unless that was something on the bottom shelf. Bending over for a closer look, he noticed a package wrapped in oilcloth, tucked away in the corner.

His heartbeat quickened. A revolver? A stash of diamonds? A skull? He took his time to unwrap the package, feeling with his fingers to rule out the gorier possibilities, and ended up with a wooden box. It was roughly the length of a ruler, and deep enough to hold jewels or gold coins or bones. He gave it a shake. Nothing rattled or clinked, but that didn't mean anything. There could be another package inside, wrapped in oilcloth. Or the box could be full of paper, like letters or thousand-dollar bills.

He took the box upstairs, enjoying the possibilities while, at the same time, preparing to be disappointed.

In the brighter light of his bedroom, he could examine the box more clearly. It had been sanded and lacquered and polished to such a sheen that it appeared to be underwater. And it wasn't made of one kind of wood, but several different kinds, cut into tiny geometric shapes and pieced together to form inlaid patterns of birds, trees, ships, and waves. The colors were all crayon shades—burnt sienna, reddish brown, golden brown, a brown so dark it looked black.

Kevin rubbed his hands together and breathed deeply. The moment had come. Tense with anticipation, he raised the lid.

"No way!" he burst out. There had to be something. A special box, the way it had been hidden, and it was empty? He shook it hard. Up, down, side to side. He examined the top, the bottom, the inside of the lid, the corners—nothing. Unbelievable.

It was definitely time for a swim. An invigorating swim with no parents hovering, a chance to work off his disappointment. He grabbed a beach towel, took an apple to eat on the way, and set off for Plover Beach.

Chapter Twelve

Plover Beach had transformed since the early hours of the morning from an empty stretch of sand to a playground of kids, dogs, teenagers, old folks, and young folks, doing whatever it was they were doing and enjoying themselves. Building sand castles, jumping the waves, eating, drinking, sunbathing, climbing rocks at the end of the beach, cannonballing from the float a few yards off the shore, waving off horseflies or sand fleas, putting on sunscreen or lounging on a beach towel reading or looking around to see who on the beach might be interesting.

The water was as cold as it had been the day before, but this time Kevin was expecting it. Besides, it was no worse than the seawater at Willows Beach or other beaches around Victoria. The trick was to run in fast before your feet got numb, duck your head under so your whole body was in cold shock, and start swimming. After the first few strokes it felt great. Refreshing. Especially on a hot afternoon.

He swam until he got tired, treaded water for a while, thought about swimming to the float later on so he could practice some dives. Too many kids there now, jumping into the water, splashing the girls, making them shriek.

He swam some more, switching from a backstroke to a crawl. If Zack were there, they'd be racing across the bay, challenging each other to swim harder and faster, and they'd float on their backs and talk about nothing or everything and go under to see who could hold his breath the longest. Kevin decided his goal for the summer would be to swim across the bay, end to end, without having to rest. His swimming instructor would be proud. Would his dad?

Man, it felt good. To be away from the flies and the crowded beach and, best of all, "we're all in it together" family time. What a relief. He'd hardly had a minute to himself since they'd arrived, and working in the basement didn't count.

He rolled over onto his back. Eyes closed, and with the sun on his face, he floated lazily, feeling himself being lulled by the motion of the water. No schedule, no list, no set time...just all the time in the world. He sighed with contentment. Summer as it was meant to be.

The kids on the float were quieter now. No more shrieking, only an occasional splash. The sounds on the beach were fading, too. Were people leaving, or was he drifting farther away?

He heard a girl call out from somewhere, "Where's Michael? What have you done?"

Kevin smiled, half-tempted to call back, "Don't know, don't care!"

A shadow passed between him and the sun, blocking the warmth and the light behind his eyelids. Not clouds, he hoped. But as suddenly as it had appeared, the shadow moved on.

At that moment Kevin felt something brush against his fingers and around his hand. Seaweed or a school of minnows? Jellyfish tentacles? More like someone's fingers.

"Hey!" He jerked his hand back and opened his eyes. He expected to see someone floating alongside, someone who'd gotten too close and whose hand had accidentally brushed against his, but there was no sign of anyone.

He made for the float, thinking it must have been seaweed. A Nova Scotia light-as-a-touch type of seaweed.

There were a few kids jumping into the water, and some older guys flirting with three girls. No one paid attention to Kevin.

If he were like Courtney, it'd be a different story. She knew how to approach people, how to say the right thing. Within minutes she'd be friends with everyone on the float and making plans to meet up the next day. Another of her many gifts that endeared her to their dad, Mr. Sociable. Well, if you had it, you had it. If not, forget it.

She'd be surprised when he showed her the box. They all would. Nobody had found a clue about Seaton, except for Kevin, and he now had two clues—the sea chest and the box. A thought struck him. What if the box was made of wreck wood? He'd seen examples in the museum in Halifax. If Seaton had made the box out of bits of wood from a shipwreck, all the more reason to think he had been a sailor.

"Hey, kid!" A boy Kevin's age was rowing toward him. "Can you grab the rope?"

Kevin took the rope and held the boat steady as the boy shipped the oars and clambered onto the float.

"Thanks," he said. He tied the rope to a cleat and sat next to Kevin. "You a CFA?" He laughed at Kevin's blank look. "A Come From Away."

"Oh yeah. Right," Kevin said, remembering that "away" meant anywhere outside Nova Scotia. "I'm from B.C.—Victoria, actually. You know, on Vancouver Island? The other coast. About as far west from here as you can get." Jeez, a geography lesson. What was he thinking? He cleared his throat, hoping that the heat flooding into his face would be mistaken for sunburn, not embarrassment. "How about you?"

"I live in town, near Fishermen's Wharf. I'm Jarrett."

"I'm Kevin. You've got an awesome boat," he said, admiring the yellow boat with green trim.

"It's a dory. And you are an awesome swimmer. I saw you earlier. That water is freezing! How can you stand it?"

Kevin shrugged. "Crazy, I guess. It's not that bad once you get in."

"You here for a while? Where you staying, in the RV park over there?" He pointed to a spot across the bay.

"We're in the house at Shearwater Point," Kevin said.

"The Seaton place? You've got to be kidding. It's supposed to be haunted. How long are you staying?"

"The whole summer. What do you mean, haunted?"

"Why, you scared?" Jarrett laughed. "It's just a rumor. Hey, you want to go for a row?"

"Seriously? Like now?"

"Yeah, c'mon. See the marina? There's a store there; we can get something to drink."

Kevin grinned. It was probably the goofy-with-pleasure grin Courtney teased him about, but what the heck, he'd made a friend.

Chapter Thirteen

Kevin tore home from the beach, bursting to tell the others about his day. They'd be back by now, and when he showed them the wooden box and told them about meeting Jarrett and finding out about Angus Seaton— well, not that much, not yet, but Jarrett's gran, who volunteered in the library, had actually known Seaton, so they had to go see her.

Spotting his parents on the verandah, he bounded up the path to join them. "Hey, guys! Where's Courtney? Wait'll you hear—"

"Where have you been?" His father was furious.

Kevin's spirits plummeted. No hope of retrieving them, not when Dad was in a state. And forget about telling him anything. He never listened.

"We leave you in charge, three hours at the most, and you take off. Did you think to leave a note? You didn't even lock the door."

"I went for a swim, okay? I didn't plan—" He swore under his breath. The beach towel. Brand new, price tag still on. He'd left it on the beach.

"That's your whole problem! You never plan, you never think past your nose, you have no sense of responsibility—and don't give me that look!"

"What look? I just sighed. I'm sorry, all right? I worked my butt off in that basement. Bet you guys stopped for ice cream in the middle of your... whatever. Don't I deserve a break?"

"Everything's fun and games with you, isn't it? Did you forget that I was arranging a truck to take away that junk? Did you think of when it might be coming, and that it might be a good idea to clear out the basement as soon as possible?" He glared at Kevin. "Right. I didn't think so."

Kevin's temper flared. "How soon? I'm not clearing out the whole basement."

"You haven't been doing much clearing at all. How much time did you spend taking off those boards?"

"A couple of minutes—jeez! Are you through yet?"

"I'm through for now. You can count yourself lucky no one came and trashed the place while you were gone."

"Don't worry about it," Courtney said later, catching up to him on the stairs.

"Where've you been?" Kevin scowled. "Thanks for coming to my rescue."

"I was in the shower. Look, I'll help with the basement. I already moved some of the boards when you were out."

"Thanks, Courtney. I owe you one."

"I saw the cupboard," she said. "Did you find anything?"

Kevin smiled, pleased that he could tell her. "I found a wooden box. Come have a look."

The box caught her attention the moment she entered the room. "It's beautiful," she said. "All these little pieces...must have taken hours to make. I bet some of this wood is mahogany. Mum or Dad might know. Have you showed them?"

"Haven't had a chance. But forget about showing Dad. I'm not even telling him."

"You should take it to a museum or an antique shop, find out if it's worth anything. Maybe it's the type of box that privateers used."

"I have a different theory," he began, and told her his thoughts about Angus Seaton.

Late that night, after everyone had gone to sleep, Kevin climbed out his bedroom window and onto the verandah roof. So Dad didn't think he planned ahead? Ha! He got down on all fours, crawled backward to the edge of the roof, and lowered himself onto the verandah railing. He jumped off, landed in a combat-style crouch worthy of any action figure, and stole down the path.

The beach was deserted, the tide going out. With an almost-full moon and only a scattering of clouds, Kevin had no trouble spotting the beach towel. Someone had thoughtfully spread it on a log above the high-water line.

He sat in the sand and leaned back against the log, the towel draped over his shoulders. He could sleep out here, fall asleep to the sound of waves. Or he could row to the float, if he had a boat, and be rocked to sleep. He had to get into the boat shed. The plan for tomorrow? Finish the basement, open the boat shed. That was in the morning. In the afternoon he'd go to the library and talk to Jarrett's gran about Angus Seaton. *See, Dad? I can think ahead.*

A movement on the water caught his attention. Was someone swimming? He thought he could make out a shape, but couldn't tell whether it was faceup or facedown. Strange...he hadn't seen anyone enter the water.

"Hey!" he called out. "Anybody there?"

No answer, but it wouldn't hurt to check. He'd have a good laugh if it turned out to be an inflatable toy some kid had left on the beach. If so, he'd put it where he'd found his towel, one good deed for another.

He was almost at the water's edge when he stopped. Had he missed something? The shape had changed. No longer floating, but standing. Standing motionless in the water, halfway between the shoreline and the float. Was it a girl? She was looking in his direction. Looking at him or through him, he couldn't tell.

"Are you okay?" he asked, taking a few steps closer.

She raised her hand, palm facing out, as if telling him to stop.

"Okay," he said. He guessed she was being cautious, and would come out of the water as soon as he left the beach. But there was something so unusual about her and the situation that he couldn't tear himself away.

Was she really there? She was almost impossible to see, the way the moon was appearing and disappearing in the clouds—light on, light off—and Kevin had to keep rubbing his eyes and adjusting his vision. She had dark hair down to her waist and was dressed entirely in black, in some long, flowing thing that covered her arms and her legs. If it weren't for her white face, she'd be invisible.

"What?" Kevin cried out, stepping forward. He thought he'd seen her lips move. "What did you say? I can't hear you!"

A sudden gust of wind stirred up the sea, causing a wave to break over his feet. He jumped out of the way, startled. When he looked back to the sea, it was empty.

Man, oh man, he thought, heading for home. What was *that* all about?

He never should have stayed out so long, staring at the sea and letting his mind wander. His head hurt, his eyes hurt, his muscles hurt—he might have overdone the swimming, been a little too vigorous with the crowbar. His face and shoulders hurt from sunburn. He needed to sleep, and not get up at dawn.

He had reached the path leading up to the house when he heard a voice behind him, so soft it might have been coming from inside his head.

Where's Michael? What have you done with my boy?

It had to be the girl. There hadn't been a sign of anyone else on the beach. And now she was following him and wanting to talk? How was he supposed to know where Michael was? He didn't even know him. "I'm too tired for this," he said, turning to confront her.

There was no one there. "Not funny!" he yelled, walking more quickly. He'd had enough.

He was rattling the doorknob, trying to open the door, when he realized something. *Where's Michael?* He'd heard it before. In the bay, floating on his back, picking up sounds, he'd heard a girl's voice saying the same thing. *Where's Michael? What have you done?*

Weird, Kevin thought. What were the odds—

"Who's there?" An angry voice from inside the house.

"It's me, Kevin." He winced, suddenly remembering that he'd gone out through his bedroom window, not through the front door. What an idiot. "I'm locked out. Sorry."

His dad flung open the door and yanked him inside. "What the hell's going on? Do you have any idea what time it is?"

"No—"

"It's three o'clock in the morning! Where have you been?"

"I left the beach towel—"

"And went back for it in the middle of the night?"

"I didn't want to let on that I forgot, okay? So I snuck out the window."

Where's Michael?

Her again. The same lilting voice, the third time in a day. "I don't know!" he said. He looked around, half-expecting to see her standing in the doorway, or outside on the verandah, hovering in the dark—

"Kevin! Look at me when I'm talking to you. You went out the window? You could have fallen and broken your neck. Did you stop and think of that?"

What have you done with my boy?

"Nothing! I mean, no, I didn't think—" He squeezed his eyes shut, as if that would block out the voices, hers and Dad's, hammering at him from two directions, outside, inside, or wherever hers was coming from. If they didn't stop—

"And you couldn't remember to come in the same way?" his father said. "No! That would've been too smart. You have to bang on the door and wake everybody—"

"I said I was sorry."

Where's Michael?

"I don't know!"

"Don't you ever think of anybody but yourself? Honestly, Kevin—"

What have you done with my boy?

"Shut up!" he shouted, clapping his hands to his ears. "I don't know what you're talking about—" He stopped, aware that he wasn't making sense. "God, Dad, I'm sorry. I don't know what I'm saying, I just want to go to bed. Please, stop. You can kill me in the morning."

He went up to his room and collapsed on the bed, desperate for sleep. But she wouldn't stop.

Where's Michael? What have you done with my boy?

On and on, like the lapping of waves on the shore, she kept on.

Chapter Fourteen

"This is what you found behind the boards? Looks like it's mostly mahogany. This part here is teak. Some bits of solid oak...not bad."

Kevin gave himself a mental high five and scored himself a point. He'd taken the box downstairs at breakfast, hoping that his dad would find it so interesting he'd forget about the night before. Judging from the way he was examining the box, it seemed to have worked.

"'Not bad,' Jim?" said Kevin's mother. "You can do better than that, can't you? That box is a work of art."

She turned and gave Kevin a warm smile. "Well done, Kevin. Your perseverance with the boards really paid off."

"Didn't I tell you?" Courtney said. "You had to show them."

"I get to keep it, remember, Dad?" He wanted to make that totally clear.

"That's what I said," his dad agreed.

"Good. Because I've got a theory about Angus Seaton. And I know about someone who knew him," he added, telling them about Jarrett and his grandmother.

"You say she volunteers at the library?" His dad looked up with interest.

"Let's go right now. It's on my list for Friday, but what the heck. Today's list can wait. We're on vacation."

Kevin grinned and scored himself another point. Good thing he'd reminded Dad of his "finders-keepers" promise. Otherwise, the way he was eyeing it, the box would have ended up on display in the living room. Instead of in Kevin's room where it belonged.

As luck would have it, the friendly volunteer who welcomed them to Ragged Harbour's tiny library was Jarrett's grandmother. "Good morning!" she said, extending a hand. "I'm Marian Nickerson and you must be Kevin. Jarrett told me about you. You're spending the summer in the old Seaton house? Wonderful! How are you all liking it?"

Her words and smile included everyone, and, for what seemed to Kevin to be an overly long time, his parents and Courtney did nothing but talk to Mrs. Nickerson about how much they were enjoying their time in Nova Scotia, the food, the beaches, the history, whatever.

Kevin finally broke in, hoping to move things along. "Jarrett said you knew Angus Seaton."

Mrs. Nickerson laughed. "Jarrett's a great one for exaggerating. I was the same age as Myles, Angus's son. Angus was at least thirty years older than me, so I can't really say I knew him. I do know a few things about him, though."

"We don't know anything about him except that there's a sea chest in the house and I found a box that could have been made out of wreck wood. So I'm wondering, was he a sailor?"

"Why yes, he was!" She gave him a look that clearly meant good for you, aren't you clever.

Three points for Kevin. He grinned at his dad, trying to look more humble than smug.

"Does that mean he found a shipwreck, or was he on one?" Courtney asked.

"Yes and no," Mrs. Nickerson said. "You've heard of the *Titanic*—"

"He was on the *Titanic*?" Kevin burst out.

"No, the *Mackay-Bennett*, a cable ship. He was part of the crew that went out to look for bodies after the *Titanic* went down. He was only seventeen at the time. Terrible thing for someone that age to have to do."

Kevin grimaced. It was one thing to think about "bodies, bodies, everywhere," or to see that sort of scene in a movie, or on the news, like after earthquakes or hurricanes or volcanic eruptions. But to haul dead bodies out of the water—how gross was that? Wouldn't they be decomposing and stinking? Wouldn't they fall apart? Yuck. His class hadn't covered that part of the disaster. They'd heard stories about survivors, but not about dead bodies. And they'd never heard about the men who'd had to pull them in, or the effect that such a grisly job would have had on them. Knowing that one of those men had been Angus Seaton, and that he was somehow connected to his own father—God.

And Kevin was living in Angus Seaton's house. Seaton could have used pieces of wood from the *Titanic* to make the box in the basement. He could have picked up the wood along with the dead bodies—"What?"

His attention snapped back to Mrs. Nickerson. "Did you just say Angus Seaton was *mad?*"

"I don't like to use that particular word, but he was different," she said. "He'd get these spells. They'd come on sudden. We'd see him on the street or on the beach, talking to himself, shouting things to people who weren't there."

"What kinds of things?" Kevin asked.

"Funny, isn't it?" his dad said. "People do the same thing nowadays, but on their cell phones."

Mrs. Nickerson laughed. "Yes, it's normal behavior to look as though you're talking to yourself these days. But at the time...I was a little girl, remember, and it scared me to see an adult acting like that. All the kids were scared of him. Our parents never let us go to Shearwater Point, and that was a shame because Myles was the nicest boy. Painfully shy, but nice. We went to school together right here in the village, but when he was ten his mum took him away. They just up and left and never came back. Angus spent time in a hospital after that, what we used to call a mental hospital."

"His son never came back, not even once?"

"Only once that I know of, and I've lived here all my life. He came back after Angus died, to see about the house. He never lived there himself, just rented it out, and he always had a property manager to look after things. Now, this could be a rumor, but I heard that Myles wasn't allowed to sell it because of something in his father's will. Can't imagine what."

"We know!" Kevin grinned. "It's because Angus—"

"He must have had a good reason," his dad cut in, shaking his head at Kevin.

"Whatever the case, Myles never contested the will."

"Can I use one of the computers?" Kevin asked. Enough about Myles and the will. If Dad didn't want to give out that Angus had left him the property, that was his business.

Time to e-mail Zack. After that he'd search for information on the *Mackay-Bennett*, find out more about the *Titanic* connection and dead bodies. No wonder Angus went mad.

He'd check out some *Titanic* websites, too, the ones he'd discovered in class. He wouldn't find Angus Seaton, but what the heck, there could be something. And while he was in the library, might as well borrow some books with the temporary card Mrs. Nickerson had offered. Maybe a book about shipwrecks on the South Shore, or a book about the *Titanic* that he hadn't already read.

Chapter Fifteen

For the next several days Kevin threw himself into the tasks at hand. His personal to-do list was shaping up. Clean out the basement? Check. Hack out brambles and bushes? Check. Family visit to the breakwater to buy lobster? Check. Learn how to pick up a lobster without losing a thumb? Check, and a photo to prove it. Flip burgers on the new gas barbecue? Check. And more photos.

Walking home from the library the day after the locked-out night, he had made an unspoken vow not to do or say anything that might irritate his dad, even though it killed him not to nag about the dory they'd found in the boat shed. The number of times he'd bitten his lip to keep from asking when he could try it out. Torture! They'd also uncovered a small dinghy, though it didn't have the same appeal.

Kevin had been hopeful when his father had gone shopping and come back with life jackets. But there they were, hanging in the shed, still waiting to be broken in.

He met up with Jarrett a few times before Jarrett went away on vacation, and made another vow—to learn how to row the dory before Jarrett came back. He was hoping they could row over to one of the many islands off Ragged Harbour.

He e-mailed Zack every couple of days, telling him about his regular swimming workouts and how Zack had better be prepared come September.

He didn't tell Zack, or anybody else, that he was hearing things. How crazy would that sound? He couldn't go to the beach without thinking of the girl he'd seen, the way she'd stood in the water, staring at him. The way she'd disappeared, only to follow him with her voice.

He hadn't seen her again, but he'd heard her. At night, when he was asleep.

Where's Michael? What have you done? What have you done with my boy?

The same lilting voice asking the same questions, making him feel more and more uneasy. When he went to bed his body grew tense, his muscles tightened, his pulse raced. He dreaded falling asleep, not knowing if he'd hear the voice or not, but it made no difference, he was always on edge. He couldn't escape it. He couldn't drive it away.

He hated that he didn't know the answers to the questions. *Where's Michael?* How was he supposed to know?

And why Kevin? Why not Dad or Mum or Courtney—but maybe they were hearing it, and didn't want to let on. Because if they told anyone, Kevin knew what the reaction would be. *You're crazy!* Why else was he keeping it to himself?

He had to ask. He would ask, and soon. He'd keep it light, like a joke. Anybody hear that girl last night? Just curious. Thought I heard something...ha-ha. Bad dream, I guess...

Had other people seen the girl, or heard her voice? People who'd been renting the house from Myles Seaton? Was that why Myles never lived in it?

But...what if it wasn't the voice that had put Myles off? What if he knew the reasons behind it? Kevin gave an involuntary shiver. *Where's Michael? What have you done with my boy ...*

What if Myles had known Michael? What if he had known the answers to the questions?

With the newspapers carted off for recycling and the yard rubbish removed, Kevin's father announced that it was time to try out the boats. Life jackets on, oarlocks and oars in place, they pushed the boats into the water. After rowing around the bay for a couple of hours, first in the dory, then in the dinghy, they judged them to be watertight.

Kevin was hopeless with the oars at first, but accepted his dad's criticism without comment. *Pull together! Not like that—no wonder you're going in circles. You've got to get into a rhythm. Pull together. Concentrate!*

His father was more excited about the dinghy. "We could attach an outboard motor and zip into town by boat. What do you say we go shop for an outboard?"

"What, you and me?"

"Sure! You can go out in the dinghy sometimes, once you get the hang of the outboard. It's a lot easier than rowing. I had a dinghy when I was a kid, at the summer cabin. Sure had some good times."

"You never told me that."

"Ancient history, right? You wouldn't be interested. But look, we'll need some new rope, an extra set of oars—let's make a list. I heard of a good marine supply store about a half hour drive from here."

"Can we get some paint for the dory? I wouldn't mind scraping it down and repainting it, if that's okay."

His father's face lit up. "You're asking me? Of course it's okay!" He tousled Kevin's hair, a sign of affection Kevin hadn't felt in ages. "What color were you thinking? Blue?"

"No, traditional colors. Yellow with green trim. Like Jarrett's dory. Remember, I was telling you about it? Anyway, you know why they use yellow and green? 'Cause yellow shows up on dark water and green shows up in white fog. Cool, eh? Jarrett told me."

"Well, you can pick any color you like."

After a quick bite of lunch, they were off. Kevin couldn't believe it.

Spending time with his dad, having something in common—he couldn't remember the last time they'd done something together, something that didn't involve soccer.

"Tell me about the boat you had as a kid," he urged. "I'm interested, honest."

And his dad told him. He talked about his summers on Pender Island, going fishing with his parents, making friends with the local kids, the camping trips on neighboring islands, the dinghy with the three-horsepower motor he'd gotten for his twelfth birthday.

"I'm telling you, Kev, I had some of the best times in that little boat. My mum taught me how to swim, but I never really took to it. Boats were more my thing. My poor mother, she'd be sick with worry, the way I used to speed around in the dinghy. Of course I could never go without a life jacket on. Rowing, that's what she liked. We'd go out on the water, seals would pop up, give us a curious look. You know, I was only sixteen when she died, same age as Courtney is now. Four years after that, Dad was gone."

"I didn't know," Kevin said. "I knew they were dead . . . it must have been tough."

"One thing they taught me? The importance of family and spending time together, 'cause it's all a part of who you are. Right, Kev? Now, how much farther have we got to go? You ready for a pit stop or a snack? Or should we wait till we get there?"

"You're asking me?"

"Well, yeah! Don't look so shocked."

Kevin grinned. "The last sign we passed said twenty kilometers, so let's keep going. Tell me more about your summer vacation. Do you have any pictures?"

"Hundreds, probably. They'd be in with my dad's papers. Photo albums, that sort of thing, all in boxes above the garage. One of these days I'll go through them, see what's there."

"I could help," Kevin offered.

His dad turned to him and smiled. "That'd be great."

Kevin felt an unexpected welling up inside. *Special.* His dad was telling him stories and making him feel special. Was this how Courtney felt all the time?

The thought of his sister prompted Kevin to bring up a decision he'd made. "Dad," he began. "I've been thinking..." Come on, Messenger, don't wimp out. Tell him you've made up your mind, no more soccer. "It's about next year—"

"Hey! Isn't that the place! They said to watch for a big shopping mall. Hang on, I've got to make a quick right. Good thing I noticed, or we would've gone past. And look, there's a café down the road. What were you saying?"

The moment had passed. "It can wait."

They bought all the items on the list, with plenty of time for a second lunch. The only thing that could have turned into an argument was the paint for the dory. A sale on white and pre-mixed blue won out over Kevin's preference of yellow and green. He didn't point out that blue and white might not be the best choices if you were on the water at night or happened to get lost in the fog.

Chapter Sixteen

Where's Michael?

Does he weep for me in the deep?
Does he walk on land, searching for me?
How will he know me? How will he know me?
Well may you sleep . . .

"Oh, no . . ." Kevin moaned into his pillow. The voice wouldn't back off. *Well may you sleep?* He hadn't slept in three weeks, not with the voice haunting him every night.

The girl, the voice—no wonder Michael, whoever he was, had gone off somewhere. If she'd been at Michael the way she was going at Kevin, he'd be going, too. Going crazy.

Does he weep for me in the deep—was that supposed to mean "water"? Did she want to know if Michael was on land or on water? But she didn't say *on the deep,* it was always *in the deep. In* the water . . . could he have drowned?

God, Messenger. Listen to yourself. Acting like there's a real Michael and you're hearing a real person, analyzing every word she's saying. Get over it.

He got up and pulled on some clothes. The sun was rising. If he went for a walk or a run he might get tired enough to fall asleep and stay asleep, at least for a couple of hours.

He crept out of the house and ran along the beach to the causeway. No one was around, the fishermen likely being out in their boats or in town with their families.

With the tide being so low and the light becoming brighter, he saw that the little island across the way was accessible. All he had to do was walk to the end of the breakwater and across the beach.

He scrambled down the buildup of boulders and picked his way across a mucky stretch of seaweed to the first of what could serve as stepping-stones—large concrete slabs encrusted with barnacles, possibly the footings from an old pier.

It was farther to the island than he'd expected. When he reached it, he climbed up a grassy slope and found a sheltered spot in the sun. Perfect.

Next high tide, he'd be able to row to the island in the dory. He thought of it with pride. It had been his project from the start, and he'd seen it through to the finish. Scraping off the old paint, sanding and sanding until his brain felt as raspy as the sandpaper, sanding until the wood felt as smooth as the wreck-wood box. He'd put on two coats of paint and had cleaned out the brushes at the end of each session. A spell of miserable weather had helped. Nothing like having a dry boat shed to keep you out of the wind, rain, sleet, and fog.

His father had given him free rein. Kevin couldn't remember the last time his dad had left him in peace to work on his own, but no doubt he had his reasons. Like secretly hoping that Kevin would fail? Would've been nice if his dad had said something besides "Not sure about the colors," especially since he was the one who had picked them out.

His always-reliable mother had praised him to an embarrassing degree. Courtney had high-fived and raved about how awesome the dory looked, and asked if Kevin would teach her to row.

He had to admit, he'd become a good rower. He could turn left or right and move in a straight line in the right direction. No more going around in circles or bashing the oars on the water or suffering his dad's barbs from the sidelines. "Not like that. How many times do I have to tell you? Pull together. You're hopeless."

He leaned back against the slope, cradling his head in his hands and gazing out to sea. Actually, things were looking good. The house was feeling more like home, the area was becoming familiar, and he knew his way around Ragged Harbour. Dozens of little islands dotted the bays around the village, and he planned to explore them all. His dad was even letting him go out in the dinghy, now that he'd learned to run the outboard. Maybe he could take the dinghy to some of the farther-out islands, buy a little tent and go camping. Maybe with Jarrett, when he got back from vacation. No sign of him yet, though.

Kevin felt like a local when he rowed to the harbor and tied up at Fishermen's Wharf. Or when he and his dad sped over in the dinghy to buy gas for the outboard motor. People who worked at the wharf or in shops around town recognized them and said hello, asked how things were going at Shearwater Point. Told them how nice it was to see the old Seaton place being occupied.

In spite of repeated visits to the library, they hadn't learned anything new about Angus Seaton. His parents had scrolled through dozens of 1912 newspapers on microfilm, Kevin and Courtney had searched *Titanic*-related websites. The stuff Kevin had discovered on the Encyclopedia-Titanica site? Stunning! He could spend hours reading the descriptions of bodies picked up by Angus Seaton and the crew. False teeth, missing teeth, bald heads, receding chins, bodies badly decomposed, dozens of tattoos like a girl's head in the center of an anchor or a snake coiled around a palm tree. Weird-sounding clothing. What were *drawers*, *truss*, or *combinations*? (Not that he really wanted to know.) A whole person reduced to a few words.

Courtney said it was ghoulish and morbid, reading that stuff. Kevin agreed. But it was helping him understand what Angus Seaton had gone through. Could a person ever get over an experience like that?

The sun was getting higher. His early morning walk had done the opposite of what he'd been hoping for. Sleep, now? Forget it. He was wide awake.

He got to his feet, stretched, and started down the slope. He was planning his day when he skidded to an abrupt stop. "You idiot!" he cried out. "How could you forget the tide?" He half-ran, half-stumbled down the rest of the slope, pounding the air and cursing himself for his stupidity. Unbelievable! Why had he stayed so long? He should have known the tide was coming in. Now he'd have to swim to shore or stay stranded until the next low tide. Swimming was no problem, except that the distance to the beach was farther than what he'd been swimming at Plover Beach, and if he swam to the end of the causeway, which appeared to be closer, he'd have to fight the current. Of all the insane—God! Dad would go ballistic with this one.

As he was weighing his options, he caught a glimpse of a concrete slab. Some of the slabs were higher than others, so if he swam to a high one... well, no point waiting any longer. He gritted his teeth and plunged in.

The shock of icy water made him gasp. He was farther out than he'd thought, and with the wind and current as well as the cold, he needed all his strength to stay on course.

A wave bashed him sideways, scraping him against a bed of razor-edge barnacles. It was a good sign, despite the pain, for the barnacles were likely attached to one of the concrete slabs. If he could get his footing, he could step along the bridge.

He treaded water, feeling around with his feet until he found a solid base and stood up. Shivering, knee deep in water, he was watching for another possible step when he saw something odd. A dark form was moving against the current, but with no apparent effort... moving toward him... a body... no... somebody floating. Rising from the water...

The girl in black.

Chapter Seventeen

Kevin felt his stomach clench. The sun was in his eyes, lighting the girl from behind, making her appear like a shadow. But she was close enough for him to see her pale face, her wide, searching eyes, her mouth half open as if she were about to speak.

Where's Michael?

Has his body been taken by the sea?

Does he weep for me in the green-black deep?

What have you done, robber of the dead?

Her arms reached out toward him.

Kevin gagged with fear, his heart pounding in his throat. The voice was the same, but the words were different. *Michael, taken by the sea…* Michael must have drowned. And the girl was blaming Kevin. She wanted to punish him. She meant to drag him under. He looked around wildly for a way to escape. Swim back to the island? Yell for help? He thought he heard an outboard motor, but couldn't see a boat. The people on the causeway were too far away. How did you escape from a ghost?

Does he walk on land, searching for me?

"I don't know!" Kevin cried in despair. She was so close this time, would she listen if he talked to her? He turned, looked to where he'd seen her face and outstretched arms, looked back to where he'd first seen her floating, looked out to the horizon and along the shoreline, but there was no sign of her, no sign that she'd ever been there. Only a white plastic bottle bobbing in the waves.

His shoulders collapsed with relief. He exhaled the biggest, deepest breath and laughed out loud, imagining how Zack would react when he told him. *A detergent bottle, and you thought it was a face? You were going to talk to it?*

He could swim to shore now, could swim twice as far if he had to, and as for the cold—what cold? Compared to the deathly cold he'd felt moments ago, he was boiling.

He was about to dive in when he heard the rumble of an engine. So he *had* heard an outboard. Better yet, a boat was coming his way. "Hey!" he yelled, waving his arms above his head. "Over here!"

The boat slowed down. "Need a lift?" An older teen held out an oar as a younger boy cut the motor.

Kevin grabbed the oar and, when the boat nudged in closer, he clambered aboard. "Thanks," he said through chattering teeth. "Thanks a lot."

The older boy pulled a blanket out from under the bow. "Take this," he said. "You must be freezing."

Kevin gratefully wrapped the blanket around himself, hugging it to his chest. So much for not feeling the cold, or thinking he could swim to shore. He was worn out and freezing, especially with the boat moving at full throttle, but freezing wasn't the half of it. Why did he have to be picked up by kids his own age? He kept his eyes lowered, embarrassed. The way they were handling the boat, they were probably locals, thinking what a screwup he was, a CFA who didn't know about tides. Had they seen him flailing around, looking as though he'd seen a ghost when it was only a plastic bottle? They'd be laughing about him later, the skinny half-drowned CFA they'd fished out of the water.

"Hey, Kevin! How you doing?"

Kevin raised his head at the sound of his name and had a good look at the boy in the stern. "Jarrett!" he said, his face cracking in a grin. "You're back from vacation? I didn't recognize the boat. Man, I'm glad to see you."

"We got back the other night." Jarrett pointed to the boy in the bow. "That's Morgan, my brother. We've been out for a spin. Hey, don't feel bad about missing the tide. Happens all the time. Where you heading? Don't tell me. Shearwater Point."

"You staying there?" Morgan laughed. "That house is haunted."

Kevin scoffed and rolled his eyes, brushing off the idea as ridiculous. He couldn't let on what he was thinking. That it might be true. There must have been something that had started the rumor. For the first time he wondered if Angus Seaton or the girl had died in the house. Mrs. Nickerson might know. He'd ask her the next time he was in the library. And what about Michael? Had he drowned, as Kevin was beginning to suspect? Another question for Mrs. Nickerson. He'd have to tell Jarrett that he'd met his gran, but later, when he didn't have to shout above the engine noise.

"Kevin!" Jarrett leaned forward. "You want to come to a beach party on Saturday? It's at our place. We do it every year."

"Sure! Thanks." It would be fun to hang out with Jarrett, and a party on Saturday, only three days away, how cool was that?

As Jarrett was guiding the boat into the bay, Kevin said, "I can swim from here. You don't have to take me all the way in."

"No problem," said Jarrett. "We're already here." He cut the engine and lifted the outboard seconds before it scraped the bottom, allowing the momentum to carry the boat up onto the sand.

"You guys sure know how to handle this thing," Kevin said. He was stepping out of the boat when Courtney appeared on the verandah.

Morgan whistled. "Who's the babe?"

"Babe?" Kevin snorted. "That's my sister, Courtney."

"Aren't you going to introduce us? Hey, Courtney!" Morgan waved. "Come to our party!"

"She doesn't like parties," Kevin said, in the faint hope that she might not have heard, or might refuse to go. He handed Morgan the blanket, thanked him and Jarrett again, and, after telling them about his dory, made plans to meet Jarrett at Fishermen's Wharf later in the day.

The next thing he knew, his parents were outside and the whole clan was gawking from the verandah. If they got invited to the party, he was staying home.

"Saturday night, Courtney!" Morgan yelled. "Kev, give us a push, we gotta go."

Kevin shoved from the bow and, with the boys pushing on the oars, the boat was soon afloat. "See you later, Jarrett!" he called, and the engine roared to life.

"A party?" Courtney said. "Sweet! You're the man, Kev."

"Oh, please." He ran past her into the house to get into some dry clothes. From his bedroom window he watched the boys running the boat in circles, bouncing over their own waves. Showing off for Courtney.

He could hear his dad below. "Who are those bozos? Did I hear something about a party? No kid of mine's going to a party with that bunch. The way they're running that boat—they shouldn't be near a boat."

"Chill, Dad. Blood pressure, remember?"

Kevin pictured his sister patting their dad on the shoulder, and gave a wry smile. He'd be hard-pressed to get permission to go to the party on his own, but if Courtney was on side? No problem.

Chapter Eighteen

Kevin stirred in his sleep. The girl in black was rising from the water, reaching out toward him.

Where's Michael?
What have you done?
What has become of my precious boy?
Has his body been taken by the sea?
Does he weep for me in the green-black deep?
Does he walk on land, searching for me?
How will he know me? How will he know me?
Well may you sleep, robber of the dead,
Thief of a lost boy's past . . .

Kevin knew he was dreaming. She couldn't grab hold of his hand or foot and pull him underwater, because he was safe in his bed. But she could make him crazy. She *would* make him crazy if she didn't stop. Her haunting voice, her endless questions—she *was* making him crazy. He woke up shivering, a cold sweat prickling his chest and back. He begged her to stop, but she wouldn't. Like an old-fashioned record with the needle stuck, she kept on and on, over and over, round and round and round.

Well may you sleep, robber of the dead,
Thief of a lost boy's past . . .

She was in the room. A black shadow, standing by the window, her face a moon in a dark sky.

"Can't you stop?" he pleaded. "Please stop . . ."

Well may you sleep, robber of the dead,
Thief of a lost boy's past . . .

He pressed his hands to his ears. Voice spinning round, room spinning round, he was going to be sick.

He got up, stumbled, and fell to his knees, crying out in alarm.

"Kevin, are you okay? Here, let me help you up." A hand reached out to him.

"Don't touch me!" he cried, scuttling backward. "I know what you're trying to do, but you can't, I won't—"

"Kevin! It's me, Courtney."

A *click*, and light filled the room.

He looked to the window. Dark blue curtains. Nothing more.

He rose shakily to his feet. "Courtney." His eyes focused on his sister. "She was standing at the window," he whispered. "The ghost . . ." He heard footsteps on the stairs and said hastily, "Don't tell Mum and Dad."

"Kevin, are you all right?" His mother flew into the room. "We heard a loud noise—did you fall? What's going on?"

"All that thumping and yelling," his father said. "It's enough to wake the dead."

"Don't say that. Don't you get it, that's the whole problem, she thinks—"

"Who, Kevin? What do you mean?"

"He was having a nightmare, Mum," Courtney said. "He's confused. Right, Kev?"

Kevin walked to the window without answering, pulled back the curtains, and looked outside. Darkness. No moon, no stars, no sign of the ghost. "I'm okay," he said. "I feel like some ice cream."

"Midnight snacks for everybody?" his father suggested. "Might as well, now that we're all up."

A few minutes later they were sitting around the table, talking and joking as if nothing had happened. Trying to include Kevin, trying to cheer him up, while skirting around the questions he knew they wanted to ask. He concentrated on his ice cream, fishing around for the peanut clusters and chocolate truffles so he could eat them before he started on the vanilla with caramel swirls. With any luck they'd all finish and go to bed, leaving him to stay up on his own. Which is what he'd had in mind in the first place. Not family time.

He knew they'd help him if they could, but how could they? They weren't hearing voices. He had asked if they were hearing unusual sounds at night or on the beach, like voices when no one was there, or if the name "Michael" had ever come up, but the answer from everyone was no.

He didn't want to answer their questions. He was sick of questions. If he told them what was happening, they'd think he was imagining things. They'd laugh it off. Or take him to a head doctor. He'd end up like Angus Seaton, in a hospital—"That's it!" he burst out, pushing back from the table. That had to be it. The ghost had driven Angus crazy.

Leaving the others in shocked silence, he hurried to his room, grabbed some paper and sprawled on his bed, scribbling his thoughts and questions. Seaton had been haunted the way he was being haunted. Why? The big question. Why him and not Dad, when Dad had inherited the house? Was there something he'd done or seen? He drew circles around the *Why*, thinking back to the first time he'd seen the ghost. The day he'd been in the basement...was it because he'd found the box? The box and the sea chest were the only personal effects of Seaton's that had turned up, and they were in Kevin's room. He couldn't prove that they'd belonged to Seaton, but so what? He couldn't prove he was hearing a ghost, either.

The next morning Kevin was up later than usual, having slept through the rest of the night. He was helping himself to some cereal when he noticed that his dad and Courtney weren't around. "Where is everybody?" he asked, joining his mum on the verandah.

When she told him they'd gone to Halifax for the day, he slammed down his bowl and said, "Why Courtney? Why couldn't I go? I could've gone back to the Maritime Museum. Jeez, Mum! Dad didn't even tell me. It's always Courtney. What are they doing, organizing a soccer team?"

"Calm down, Kevin. If you want to be mad at somebody, be mad at me. I told your dad not to wake you. You needed the sleep."

He had to admit that she was right. "Yeah... but I wanted to go to the museum in case they had something on Angus Seaton, the time he was picking up bodies."

"That's one of the things your dad's planning to do in Halifax. Not at the museum, but at the provincial archives."

"I could have helped," Kevin said grudgingly. He thought for a moment. "You know what, Mum? I bet they won't find anything. I'm going to talk to Mrs. Nickerson. Because this whole thing about Seaton and the connection to Dad? I think the answer is right here."

He left for the library after breakfast and wasted no time in putting his questions to Mrs. Nickerson. He started with the first on his list. "Did Angus Seaton die in the house?"

"No, not at all. Didn't I tell you? Angus drowned. About thirty years ago. He rowed out into Shearwater Bay. He was always out in his dory, the one you were telling me about, I suppose, the one you fixed up. Always out on the water, rowing for the exercise, I guess. But that one time, he never came back. There wasn't a storm, nothing like that, but a couple of days later his body was found, washed up on a beach. The dory was found not far off."

"Was it an accident?" Kevin wondered if Angus had seen the ghost, maybe stood up and lost his balance... or crashed into something because he wasn't paying attention.

"It didn't look like it," she said. "There wasn't a scratch on the dory, nothing to show it'd hit anything, and the oars were in the bottom of the boat, lined up side by side as neat as can be. Can you figure that? I'd be willing to bet that he took his own life."

Kevin thought for a moment. "I've got another question. This may sound stupid, but were there ever any rumors about Angus seeing a ghost?"

"Oh, gosh!" She threw back her head and laughed. "This is Nova Scotia, honey! We're full of ghosts. I know people who've seen them, my own mother included. A history as old as ours—"

"So that's a yes?" Kevin said excitedly. It was all he could do to keep from blurting out that he'd seen a ghost, but there were other people in the library, and no way did he want to appear demented.

"I'd bet my life on it," she said. "Remember I told you how Angus would talk to himself, or shout at people who weren't there? Well..." She nodded, giving Kevin a what-do-*you*-think look.

He nodded in return. "He was talking to a ghost. He could see it, but nobody else could."

"He probably saw more than one ghost, after what he'd been through."

"Yeah..." If Angus had been unhinged to start with, seeing the ghost and hearing her voice—no wonder the poor guy ended up taking his own life.

"Did you ever hear of a person called Michael? He might have drowned around here, or maybe lived in the house?"

"Not that I know of, unless you're confusing the name Michael for Myles. Sorry, I'm drawing a blank on that one."

"Did anyone die in the Seaton house?"

"Another blank, I'm afraid."

"That's okay. I've got enough information for now. Just one more thing. Do you have any books about ghosts?"

"I can definitely help you with that. Let's have a look."

Armed with a book on ghosts, he started for home.

He didn't have all the answers, but he knew a lot more than he had before. That stuff about ghosts, for instance. While Mrs. Nickerson was looking for the book she had in mind, she'd told him that ghosts usually had "unfinished business." He couldn't remember exactly how she'd described it—he'd find out more when he read the book—but the "unfinished business" made sense.

The girl was haunting him the way she had haunted Angus, because she wanted to find out about Michael. Whatever had happened to her "precious boy," she blamed them. Used words like "thief" and "robber of the dead"—oh, God. Kevin froze. He thought back to the *Titanic*. The victims' bodies...

Forget about the *Titanic*, he told himself. There's nothing to connect the ghost or Michael with the ship, nothing in the words he heard at night. "Robber of the dead"? Heck, people died all the time.

One thing he was sure of. To be free of the voice, he had to give the ghost what she wanted. He had to find out about Michael.

Chapter Nineteen

The Nickersons' annual beach party was at full throttle by the time Kevin and Courtney arrived. There were two parties, one on the beach for the older kids and teenagers, and one in the front garden for grown-ups and little kids, with a lot of coming and going between the two. Kevin almost choked when Jarrett's mum asked why he and Courtney hadn't brought their parents. It was a wonder that he wasn't sent back to get them.

The house was big and rambling and the beach was as great as the one at Shearwater Point, only it had a wharf where Jarrett and Morgan could fish and jump into the water and tie up their boats. Around the corner was Fishermen's Wharf, and the village was only a couple of blocks away.

They'd no sooner arrived when some of the teenagers, including Morgan and Courtney, ran down to the hard sand and started kicking a soccer ball around. Kevin and Jarrett were talking about their favorite DVDs when Kevin saw the ball flying up the beach toward him and, without thinking, kicked it out of the way. Kicked it so hard it sailed over everyone's head and landed in the water.

"Did I do that?" Kevin's jaw dropped.

"Way to go, Kev!" Morgan yelled. The other kids did the thumbs-up, cheering thing, and raced in to retrieve it.

Jarrett slapped him on the back. "Awesome, man! You never told me you played soccer."

"Wait till I tell Dad!" Courtney said, giving him a high five.

"Don't even mention it." Secretly Kevin was pleased. He knew she'd tell, and do a bit of bragging on his behalf. He wouldn't admit that he'd kicked the ball only because he hated the sight of the thing and resented the way it had butted into his conversation. And he was still irritated by the two soccer buddies going off to Halifax without him. It must really have been their idea to let him sleep, not Mum's. He could've slept in the car if they were so concerned about his health.

"Feel like a hot dog?" Jarrett said. "We've got tons of food and a fire pit."

Kevin followed him to a picnic table loaded with marshmallows, soft drinks, chips, nachos, every possible kind of junk food, and stuff for making s'mores. He decided to start with a hot dog and sample everything else on the table before the sun went down.

He was talking to Jarrett and his friends about an overnight camping trip when Courtney interrupted with a pointed remark about the time.

"Do you mind?" Kevin said. "We're right in the middle of something."

"Sorry, but it's time to go."

"What, already?" At least Courtney had lowered her voice so the other kids wouldn't think he was a total dork, but to strut over like a babysitter? "We just got here."

"I know you don't want to leave," she said, "but we have to be home by eleven. Haven't you noticed the time?"

"No, actually. Does it matter? When were you ever home by eleven?"

"That's different. Come on. We gave our word."

"Forget it. You're not my babysitter. If it wasn't for me, you wouldn't have even known about the party."

"True, and I'm totally grateful. Look, if you—"

"Hey, you guys aren't leaving?" Morgan appeared just then with some bottles of apple cider, one of which he offered to Courtney. "The party's just getting started."

"No, thanks." She waved the bottle away and gave Kevin a don't-even-think-about-it look.

"Try it, Courtney," Morgan said. "You, too, Kev. It's not alcoholic. My uncle's got an orchard, and we make it from his apples. It's wicked."

"I'll try one." Kevin returned Courtney's look with a try-and-stop-me glare. What was the problem? The cider wasn't alcoholic. It tasted like zesty apple juice. Way better than the watered-down wine his parents gave him to drink on special occasions. As for Courtney, who knew what went on at the parties she went to? He'd bet anything she wasn't Miss Perfect all the time.

"Stunning!" he said, clinking bottles with the others. Loud music, goofing around, talking with the local kids—he felt like an insider, not some CFA.

"Kevin?" Courtney took her flashlight from her pocket. "Did you remember to bring your flashlight, or do you want mine? Stay if that's what you're doing, but I'm keeping my word."

"If you want to stay later, I could run you back in the boat," Morgan suggested. "Get you home in five minutes."

"Okay, Courtney?" Kevin jumped at the offer. "We can both go back in the boat. You shouldn't walk home by yourself."

Instead of agreeing, Courtney seized his arm with the grip of a hawk and pulled him away from the others. "I'm responsible for you. I promised I wouldn't let you do anything stupid."

"Get off my back." He yanked his arm away. "I don't need three parents. I can be responsible. I'm having fun, for once, and that Seaton house is freaking me out. It's haunted."

"We know, Kevin." Courtney rolled her eyes.

"I'm not kidding. I hate sleeping there. I might stay here all night."

"Oh, grow up! What do you want me to tell Dad?"

"Tell him whatever you like. I don't care."

"He'll kill you if he knows you've been drinking."

"It's cider, Courtney. You know, like apple juice?"

"If you believe that—"

"Have you even tried it? You're being rude." He let out a loud belch, turned on his heel, and rejoined the group. "Sisters," he said dismissively. "You're lucky if you don't have one." He tossed his bottle into the recycling bin and looked for another cider.

He was helping himself when Morgan came up. "Is your sister walking back alone?"

"Yeah. Stubborn, eh?"

"Not smart, man. It's safe around here, but still. Girl out on her own, late at night. Don't you know anything?" He picked up his jacket and went off in Courtney's direction.

No, not smart. Kevin had noticed the way Morgan had been looking at Courtney, and the thought of her trying to shake him off if he persisted in walking her home ... but hey, Kevin wasn't her babysitter. And he'd told her not to go by herself. What else could he do? It was her choice. Nothing to do with him.

Not long after Morgan left, the party began to wind down. Parents from outside Ragged Harbour came down from the house to collect their kids for the drive home; a few older kids strolled away in pairs. Kevin lingered behind, helping Jarrett put out the fire and carrying the leftover food to the house.

He was passing the kitchen when he spotted a familiar face. "Hi, Mrs. Nickerson," he said.

"Kevin! I was hoping to see you." Wiping her hands on a tea towel, she came out to join him. "You were asking about a 'Michael'? It came to me the other night, the day after I saw you at the library. The story goes that Angus Seaton was in the village one day and he saw our neighbor's little boy in a pram, sitting outside one of the shops. Well, he made such a fuss, leaning over the boy and saying things like 'Michael! You're Michael! I've been looking for you for years.' None of it made any sense, because the boy's name wasn't Michael and he was only about two. The worst of it was, Angus started to take the pram away. Well, the mother, Mrs. Jeffreys, she tore out of that shop so fast and so mad, my mum said that Angus was lucky Mrs. Jeffreys didn't kill him."

"I never thought of Michael as a baby," Kevin mused.

"My mum was in the shop with Mrs. Jeffreys at the time," Mrs. Nickerson went on. "She saw it happen, not me. So you're not getting it firsthand. What Angus was thinking, trying to go off with that little boy, that's anybody's guess.

"Funny I remembered after all this time. Your questions are taking me back." She winked at Kevin. "Next time I see you, I might have dredged up some more. Do you need a lift home?"

He thanked her for the offer, but said he didn't mind the walk. He had a lot on his mind.

Chapter Twenty

Michael, a baby? Kevin hadn't thought of that possibility. He'd never thought of Michael as having any particular age. But a two-year-old? Okay, not exactly a baby, but close enough. No wonder the ghost had unfinished business. Losing a baby...

As for Angus Seaton, no wonder people thought he was crazy. Trying to make off with a little kid, thinking he was somebody else.

He quickened his pace to a run, anxious to get home and tell everybody about Mrs. Nickerson's story. It told more about Angus Seaton than what Dad had found in the archives, which was exactly nothing.

Where's Michael?

What has become of my precious boy?

"Not now!" Kevin cried. Couldn't he be left alone for once?

He ran faster, looking ahead to where the beach ended and the path to the house began, looking ahead to the light shining through the trees, the verandah light left on for him to see his way home.

Does he weep for me in the green-black deep?

Does he walk on land, searching for me?

How will he know me? How will he know me?

"Shut up!" So what if Michael was a baby? Sure, it was sad, but what was Kevin supposed to do about it? Nothing changed. The girl's voice was still hounding him, her ghost was still tracking him. He could sense it hovering close by, floating on the water, lurking on the shoreline. . . .

He refused to look out at the sea. He ran up the path, his stomach heaving from too much apple cider and junk food, his breath coming in painful gasps.

Well may you sleep, robber of the dead,
Thief of a lost boy's past . . .

"Go away!" he pleaded, verging on tears. "Go back to wherever . . . oh, for God's sake, please stop . . ."

He climbed the steps to the verandah, babbling about the girl, her voice and her words, accusing him, holding him responsible. *"It wasn't me!"* he shouted in despair. *"I'm not responsible!"*

"You can say that again. What's going on with you?"

"Dad!" Kevin welcomed the sound of his father's voice, the way it brought him sharply into the here-and-now. "Dad, I have to tell you, I found out—" His words were cut off as his dad hauled him inside. "What did I do now?" he said.

"Do you know what time it is?"

Kevin looked at his watch. "11:11? No, wait." He couldn't see clearly. Was it eleven past eleven or eleven past one? He hadn't realized how tired he was. "I'm on time . . . aren't I? Courtney said we had to go, so we went."

"Don't lie to me. You think Courtney didn't tell us?"

"Where is she? Is she okay?"

"She's asleep! It's after one o'clock in the morning and of course she's okay, why wouldn't she be? Morgan walked her home two hours ago, which was when you were supposed to be home."

"You met Morgan? Did you—"

"What's the idea, Kevin? Did you ever stop to think we might be worried? Ever think of making a phone call? I've been out looking for you. You could have been run over—"

"One o'clock? It's not really after one o'clock, is it? I didn't know, honest. I better...get to bed."

His father's mouth tightened. "Who do you think you are?"

Kevin was taken aback. What kind of question was that? "I'm Kevin Messenger." He tried to suppress a giggle and failed. "Who do you think *you* are?"

He could feel his veins throbbing. His stomach twisted. His dad's face swam before his eyes. He closed them and pressed his fingers to his temples, suddenly deflated. "You win, okay? I don't care. Please...leave me alone." *Real voice, unreal voice, questions, questions, where was he, who was he, where was Michael, why should he care, questions he couldn't answer, and why was Dad always so angry...*

He went into the kitchen, where his mother was getting some water.

"Mum? I thought you were asleep."

"Hardly, with all the shouting going on." She gave him a stern look. "You really let us down, Kevin, especially Courtney. Was it too much to ask that you leave the party with her and be home by a certain time?"

"Jeez, Mum." Not her, too. "It's not what you think. I found out some stuff, okay? About Angus Seaton. He drowned. Did I tell you? And Michael...I don't feel so good. My head's killing me."

"No wonder," his dad said, joining them. "What were you thinking?"

"Not now, Jim. He's going to bed. We'll have it out in the morning." She handed Kevin some water and a headache tablet and helped him to his room. "Do you remember what you were drinking at the party?"

"Didn't the babysitter tell you?" he said, flaring up again. "Apple cider, nonalcoholic. You think it matters? Leave me alone!"

He slammed the door after her and lay down.

A minute later the voice started in.

Well may you sleep, robber of the dead...

"Shut up!" Kevin shouted, bolting from the bed. "You goth freak—"

Thief of a lost boy's past...

"NO!" he erupted. He grabbed the nearest object and hurled it across the room, hollering, "STOP! Stop it stop it stop it—"

"Kevin, what's wrong? What's happening?"

"Nothing!" he raged. Mum, Dad, Courtney—the last thing he needed was to have them gaping at the door. "Nothing, nothing, nothing, leave me alone. Go on, go!" He closed the door on them, leaned against it, his chest heaving. "It's okay," he said, forcing himself to lower his voice, to be calm. "It's okay, I can handle it..."

He slouched to the floor and gazed blankly across the room. The object he'd thrown had missed the window, but another few inches and it would have gone through. He sharpened his gaze. "Oh God, no," he groaned. Not the wreck-wood box.

He choked back a sob. Of all the things he could have thrown, why that? It was ruined. A heap of broken bits of wood...he frowned. Where had the little leather purse come from? He crossed the room in one step, brushed away the debris, and picked up the purse. Black leather, worn smooth and soft, no bigger than the palm of his hand. And there was something inside.

A miniature picture frame. A double frame, held together by two hinges and a clasp that had somehow stayed intact.

He fumbled with the tiny clasp. The frame could be empty, but somehow he doubted it. A picture of Angus Seaton would be a find, a face to go with the name.

The clasp undone, he opened the frame. Sucked in a breath, and reeled with shock. Not because of the black-and-white photos inside, but because of the words written across the bottom.

Annie and Michael, our precious boy
April 2, 1912

Chapter Twenty-One

"No way," Kevin whispered. His eyes moved from the words to the photographs, one showing a woman and a baby, the other showing the baby alone. "It can't be."

The glass covering the photographs had cracked when it hit the wall, but he could still make out the images. If the baby in the picture—"our precious boy"—was Michael, then the woman was...his mother? She looked so young, seated on a chair with Michael in her lap. Michael, fair-haired, looking more like a girl in the long white gown he was wearing. Old-fashioned clothing, old-fashioned looks. Like the solemn expression on his mother's face.

If she had been smiling, Kevin considered, he probably wouldn't have recognized her. Her eyes would not have looked so unsettling, the way they stared into the camera as if they could sear a hole in the lens and look through to the other side. Kevin shuddered. Straight through to him. The way she'd looked at him before. The girl in black, like in the photograph. *Annie.* Now a ghost.

Kevin turned off the light and lay down, overwhelmed by what the photos might mean. Man, oh man—he had to put it out of his mind, at least for a couple of hours so he could—what, sleep? What a joke. Now he had not only Annie's ghost and voice to haunt him, he had her picture.

No wonder he hadn't found it before, the way it had been hidden. When Seaton was making the box—and Kevin was convinced that it had been Seaton—he must have built a false bottom. A secret compartment that had held the purse and picture frame so snugly they hadn't budged when the box was shaken.

Kevin couldn't help but admire the guy. Talk about cunning. But at the same time, how...disturbing. Creepy, even. The whole business was creepy. One secret hidden inside another and another, beginning with a boarded-up wall in the basement. And even that had been hidden behind the stacks of newspapers.

But was that the beginning? Angus Seaton must have had a reason for hiding the photographs, and his reason could have started far beyond the walls of the house.

One secret inside another. Kevin leaped out of bed, his mind racing. What if there was something more in the picture frame? Like those Russian dolls that nested inside each other—there was always a smaller one, and a smaller one after that. There could be another photograph, or something written on the back. He was starting to remove the photo of Michael when he saw some paper stuck in behind. "I knew it, I *knew* it..." With trembling fingers he pried out the paper.

He knew at once that it was not a photograph. Too thin, for one thing. And it had been folded small to fit behind the photograph, as though it had been put in for backing.

Kevin unfolded the paper and gasped. This wasn't just any paper. It was the birth certificate of Michael McConnell.

CERTIFICATE OF BIRTH

Issued: *July 15, 1911*
Name: *Michael John McConnell*
Place and Date of Birth: *Belfast, July 11, 1911*
Mother: *Annie McConnell, Belfast, County Antrim, Ulster*

AGE: *17*
FATHER: ~~unknown~~ *John Edward Collins, Belfast, County Antrim, Ulster*
AGE: ~~unknown~~ *22*

"Un-flipping-believable," he murmured. Wait till he showed the others. The satisfaction of I-told-you-so moments? Totally sweet. Not yet, though. Not until he figured out what it all meant.

As far as he could tell, whoever had replaced the word "unknown" on the birth certificate was the same person who had printed the names and date on the photographs. It must have been Annie McConnell. The printing on the rest of the certificate looked official. Why had the official or whoever put "unknown"?

Because . . . even though Annie knew who the father was, she hadn't wanted to give his name. At first. Later, for some reason, she had changed her mind.

Uncover one secret, discover another. Find one answer, end up with more questions. The biggest one being: What did Annie and Michael have to do with Angus Seaton?

All at once Kevin had it. Okay, it was only a theory, but it worked. Michael was born July 11, 1911. Seven-eleven, easy to remember. The date on the photograph was April 2, 1912. When did the *Titanic* sail? April 10. Who was picking up the dead? Angus Seaton. What were some of the personal effects found on victims' bodies? Miniature picture frames and leather purses. Kevin had seen that for himself on the *Titanic* websites.

Sure, it was unlikely, and he could be jumping to conclusions, but at least the dates made it possible. Angus Seaton could have been a "robber of the dead."

Chapter Twenty-Two

Shearwater Point, April 15, 1952

Bodies, bodies, everywhere.

That's what Angus remembered if anyone asked. And they were always asking. Every anniversary of the *Titanic* they'd come snooping around, newspaper and radio reporters, asking the same questions. "What was it like, Mr. Seaton? Anything in particular that you remember?" There were things Angus had a good mind to tell them, none of them polite. So he said what he always said.

Bodies everywhere, and the crew of the *Mackay-Bennett* bringing them in. Bodies on stretchers carried down the gangway, bodies in coffins removed by crane. One by one, each body numbered, some identified but mostly not, one hundred ninety bodies, three and a half hours to take them ashore until finally the decks were clear and the *Mackay-Bennett* went back to being a cable ship.

Leaving the ship on that sunlit morning of April 30, 1912, Angus believed the ordeal was over. He didn't know what the older men knew, that an experience like the one they'd been through, there'd be no getting over it, not for good. Sooner or later it would creep up from behind like an unexpected fog, take hold of you in its clammy grip—you and whatever was keeping you afloat—until, in the end, you would lose your way.

Bodies, bodies, everywhere...but for Angus, there was only one, the body of the girl.

He thought he'd forgotten about her. He thought he'd forgotten the day he'd brought her into the cutter. He thought he'd forgotten the events that followed.

Everything he thought he'd forgotten came back after Myles was born.

From then on, the girl's haunting face and voice were everywhere. Day and night, on land and water, she was no longer a canvas-shrouded body but a restless and demanding ghost.

Where's Michael?

What have you done with my precious boy?

He had never spoken about the girl. Never told a soul how he'd struggled to bring her into the cutter, how he'd grabbed her small leather purse before it hit the water. How he'd put it in his pocket and forgotten to turn it in to be recorded and bagged. He'd intended to give it to the duty officer, he'd been on his way to do that very thing. But then there'd been that trouble with the stack of bodies, and after that it was one thing after another, and the next day it was too late to turn it in. He was afraid of the consequences. And after days and weeks it was later still, and before long it was better to remain silent. Or so he thought.

His mind tormented him.

If he hadn't kept the purse...

If he hadn't looked inside and found the picture frame...

For over fifteen years the purse had lain at the bottom of his sea chest. Why couldn't he have let it be?

If he hadn't seen the photographs...

If he hadn't read the names...

But he had.

And no one could know.

If it wasn't the ghost tormenting him, keeping him awake at night, it was his own mind. What if little Myles discovered that his own father had robbed the dead? It was a crime. Angus could be sent to jail. What would become of Lucy and Myles if that were to happen?

Myles was at the curious age, following Angus around, asking questions. What are you doing now, Dad? Can I watch? What are you making? Can I help? Where did you get the box, Dad? What's inside? Can I look inside?

Nothing, no, nothing, no, never mind, nothing, no...

Angus knew that sooner or later Myles would sneak down to the basement and look around. He'd discover the secret and ask questions. He'd tell Lucy and she'd ask questions. The last thing Angus needed was more questions. Didn't he get enough from the girl? The same questions, over and over, and he always gave the same answers, but she wouldn't listen.

Where's Michael?

What has become of my precious boy?

Does he weep for me in the green-black deep?

Does he walk on land, searching for me?

How will he know me? How will he know me?

One day while out picking up driftwood, Angus heard the voice and exploded with rage. "Where's Michael? I keep telling you, he's dead!" Why wouldn't she listen?

Knowing that Lucy was in the village and Myles was at school, Angus stormed into the house, raging with frustration. "Where's Michael? He's in the ground, he's not walking around searching for you or anybody else."

Still shouting, Angus tore downstairs to Lucy's preserving cupboard, swept the shelves clean of preserves—never mind the broken glass and sticky jam mess on the floor—and put his wreck-wood box inside.

Thank God he'd had the foresight to hide the purse with its damning pictures. The hidden drawer so cunningly designed and crafted, though he'd made it for an altogether different purpose, had been a stroke of genius.

Well may you sleep, robber of the dead...

"I'm done with you, Annie. I'm putting you away, you and your voice and your precious boy. You want Michael? He's in the ground like thousands of others. You think he's special? You think you're the only one who's suffered? Oh, I could tell you a thing or two...."

The disasters he'd been through, the bodies...How young he'd been on the *Mackay-Bennett*, thinking that the ordeal would be over after the last coffin was removed from the ship, after the crew had buried the unknown child they'd pulled aboard the cutter. Angus had attended the memorial service, he'd seen the little boy, two years at the most, laid out on a bed of roses in his small, white casket. He'd seen the casket carried to the horse-drawn hearse, and he'd accompanied it from the church to the cemetery. The heaps of bouquets on top of the casket, the crowds lining the streets, he'd never seen the like. "It was Michael, dammit!" he burst out. "Do you hear me, Annie? Body No. 4 was Michael!"

Cover up the cubbyhole, board it up. Nails, more nails, more boards...

Disaster after disaster, bodies and bodies, and the *Titanic* victims only the start.

Bodies in the wrecks of ships sunk by the Germans, some of his own shipmates among them. Bodies in the muddy trenches of the Western Front, bodies he had never seen for himself, but no need, not with his mind haunting him with their images. Bodies by the thousands, the millions, in that terrible war. "And you think you're special, Annie?" Another outburst, more nails hammered into the ghost.

And during that same war, bodies in the streets of Halifax after the Explosion in the harbor, and him being far from home, receiving the telegram, reading the accounts in the newspapers. Bodies numbering upward of sixteen hundred at first, but rising, rising, as hundreds more were recovered.

He'd been spared the ordeal of recovering those bodies, unlike the soldiers and sailors who'd been in Halifax at the time. Spared in a physical sense...but mentally? Oh no. His mind had dragged him there, day and night, digging bodies out of the wreckage, bagging and tagging alongside the others, knowing the system by heart, for wasn't it the same as they'd used on the *Mackay-Bennett*? Personal effects placed in canvas bags, and him having to claim those of his parents when he returned to the ravaged city after the war. Paying his respects to Sarah's parents, receiving from them the engagement ring Sarah had been wearing when she died, the little ring among her other effects, bagged and tagged...his darling girl. Oh, the look on her face when she'd opened the secret drawer of his wreck-wood box and discovered the ring, its small diamond twinkling, her initials engraved with his on the inside of the band.

"You think you've suffered, Annie?" He hammered more nails, more boards, hammered until his wrist ached. "By God, you didn't live long enough to suffer. You think you're special? You think you're the only ghost?"

God, if he could shut away his thoughts with boards and nails, or throw them into the sea as he'd done with Sarah's ring, thinking it would help him get over his loss.

Fair enough that Annie couldn't get over hers, but why was she dragging him into it? Why couldn't she be grateful that Michael had had a Christian burial? Why couldn't she leave Angus in peace?

More boards, more nails...If Myles decided to have a look he'd have his work cut out for him, but by God, that would never happen. More boards, more nails. "Do you hear that, Annie? Do you hear the pounding? It's you I'm boarding up. It's you I'm hammering at, by God!"

The task completed, he fled from the house and into his dory. He had to get away, get moving, out and into the bay. Rowing, rowing in circles, the one thing that helped when the voice got too bad, and he could keep it up for hours.

A spell, Lucy called it. *Don't disturb your father, Myles, he's having one of his spells.*

Once, Angus overheard Myles tell Lucy, "The boys at school don't believe me when I say it's a spell. They say it's a fit. They say he's a lunatic and should be locked up."

Another time, Angus heard Myles telling Lucy that he loved his dad most of the time. But when he was having a spell, Myles was afraid.

Angus's heart ached to hear his son talk like that. And the time when Myles was passing the butcher's on the way home from school and saw his father smiling at a baby in a pram, saying, "There you are, Michael! Let's get you home to your mother." And Myles gaping in horror as his father began to push the pram down the street. And the baby's mother, shrieking like a witch, running after Angus and attacking him with her handbag the way one would go at a rabid dog. And if that wasn't bad enough, Angus looking over and seeing Myles, seeing that Myles had been watching.

Then there was the day that everything changed. The day that Myles came home from school and saw his father rowing in the bay, heard him shouting at someone no one else could see, the way he did during his spells. With his mother away in the village, Myles had the house to himself. He thought he had all the time in the world.

But Angus came back too soon.

He found Myles, crowbar in hand, throwing his ten-year-old body into the effort of prying off the boards, humming to himself, and Angus was on him so fast, grabbed the crowbar and, without thinking, struck the boy and knocked him to the floor.

"Look what you made me do, you wicked girl," Angus sobbed, cradling the boy in his arms. "I swear to God, you'll not have my boy. . . ."

And there's Lucy home. Seeing her boy in the arms of that madman of a husband, she's screaming and screaming, and before Angus realizes what's happening, she's taken Myles and left for good, leaving Angus to be haunted by her screaming and Myles's humming and always, always, the plaguing, festering voice of the ghost.

No wonder the villagers whispered behind his back. The nicest man on his good days, but a little unhinged, shell-shocked in the war, and that terrible loss he suffered in the Halifax Explosion . . . is it any wonder he has his spells? His mind never the same after that. And to top it off, his wife moving away with the boy . . .

They could think up a million reasons, each one a just cause for his madness and each one contributing to it. But Angus would never tell the true cause.

As he grew older he understood the gravity of what he had done. He had robbed a child and his mother of the dignity of having their names inscribed on their graves. He'd committed a crime. He'd pay for it in his own way. Annie's ghost was the albatross around his neck, and he'd carry it until the day he died or until he was able to make atonement. God willing, that day would not be long in coming.

Meanwhile, he carried on in his own peculiar way. A phone call from Myles every Christmas, the odd church supper or sailors' reunion, passing the time with the local fishermen, but mostly he kept himself to himself. He made a point of visiting Fairview Lawn Cemetery whenever he was in Halifax, to lay flowers on his parents' graves and on Sarah's. He'd never felt the same toward Lucy. No, Sarah was the love of his heart. Close to her grave was the empty plot where his weary bones would one day come to rest. In peace, God willing.

After that, he would go to another part of the cemetery to pay his respects to the *Titanic* victims. He owed them that much.

The "unknown child," for instance. Who else could he be but Michael? His grave a memorial to all the children who had perished that fateful night.

Chapter Twenty-Three

Kevin ran downstairs and into the kitchen, unable to contain his excitement. "You won't believe what I found! You know the wreck-wood box? Wait'll you see what was stashed inside. It's incredible." He pushed aside the breakfast things and placed the picture frame and birth certificate on the table. "There's Annie, before she was a ghost, and there's Michael. I told you I keep seeing her and hearing her, and don't you think it's more than a coincidence that I hear about Michael before I even find his picture and his birth certificate? And in Angus Seaton's house? Hidden, so nobody could find them? Think about it. And you know how Angus tried to steal a baby because he thought it was Michael?"

His parents and Courtney exchanged skeptical glances and gave Kevin blank looks.

"Where did you hear that?" Courtney asked.

"I thought I told you—can I have some of those pancakes?" He'd been about to say "last night" but changed his mind. Better to avoid that subject.

He paused long enough to help himself to pancakes, and went on. "Okay, are you with me? Wait till you hear my theory. This whole weird thing about Angus Seaton? I think I've figured it out." He took a couple of mouthfuls, watching as the others examined the birth certificate. He tapped the date the photographs were taken. "April 2, 1912. What happened in April 1912? The *Titanic* sank."

"And you figure that Annie and Michael were on the *Titanic*?" Courtney said. "That's a big leap, isn't it? Just because the date is April 1912."

"It's a theory, Courtney. Let's say Annie McConnell—see, there's her name on the birth certificate—let's say she was on the *Titanic*, and before she left she had the photographs taken—"

"To give to somebody," Kevin's mum suggested. "So they wouldn't forget her and Michael. And the way she wrote 'our precious boy,' I'd say the 'our'. . ."

". . . must have been directed to the father." His dad looked up from the birth certificate. "Suppose Annie McConnell—and I mean the person, Kevin, not your 'ghost'—suppose she tried to give Michael's father the photograph but he didn't want it."

"Could be," Courtney said. "Or what if his family ordered him not to have anything to do with Annie or the baby because. . . I don't know, some reason." She shrugged. "They could have been from a different social class. Star-crossed lovers, like Romeo and Juliet. How's that for a theory?"

Kevin had been listening with a degree of annoyance. Wasn't it his theory they were supposed to be listening to?

"One thing we're forgetting," his mum said. "How did these things end up here?"

"I can tell you," Kevin began, "if you'd let me finish my theory—"

"Kevin, hold on for a minute," his dad interrupted. "This is fascinating material and it may actually mean something, but let's not get carried away. We've got some unfinished business to talk about, remember? Last night."

Kevin winced. Now, right in the middle of his stunning breakthrough, Dad had to interrupt with that?

His throat tightened and his face became hot, sure signs of a flare-up that would lead to another confrontation if he wasn't careful. He had to think.

The party. Not coming home with Courtney and missing the curfew.

There'd been so much going on before and after he'd gone to his room, he hadn't given the matter a single thought. Thinking about it now, he remembered what Mum had said in the kitchen. He was always letting Dad down. Mum, too, most likely, but she had never said it to his face. Not the way she had last night.

He turned his attention to her. "I'm sorry I let you down, Mum. You, too, Courtney. I'm sorry I missed the curfew. Honest. I told Courtney why I didn't want to come home. It's really been getting to me, staying in this house. But it's going to be fine, you know why? Because I've found Michael. So Annie won't be bothering me anymore."

"Listen to yourself!" his dad said. "Don't you know how worried we are? We think it's time you saw a doctor. I've got the name of a good one in Halifax—"

"I'm not going to any head doctor! And let me finish about last night."

"Kevin, it won't do you any harm. We've made an appointment—"

"Forget it! Jeez, you wanted to talk about last night, so let me finish. I talked to Mrs. Nickerson—that's the reason I was so late—and she told me about Angus trying to steal a baby that he thought was Michael... Oh, never mind. God, I'm wiped." He lowered his head into his hands and took a few deep breaths. "There are ghosts, you know," he muttered. "Didn't we hear enough about them on those walking tours and museum tours?"

His father remained silent.

"Dad?" He looked up to see his dad gazing at the birth certificate. Showing interest? Thinking of something else? Kevin decided not to ask. "Can I be excused? I don't mind being grounded. I deserve it." He got up without waiting for a response, and started to clear the table. "Mum, I'll do the dishes. Then I have to use the laptop, if that's okay."

"My father's name was Michael," his dad said, as if he hadn't heard Kevin. "I can't remember when he was born."

"Have you got his birth certificate?" Kevin asked. "We could start doing a family tree."

His father laughed. "Dig up some family ghosts, you mean?"

Kevin bristled. "It was just an idea."

"A good one," his dad conceded. "If I ever get around to going through his papers. They've been boxed up for years, up above the garage. Didn't have the heart to go through them right after he died, and that was years ago. Later on, I forgot. So much old history…" He shrugged, dismissing the subject. "Now, we better get a move on. Laura? What time did Morgan say they were coming?"

She looked at her watch. "About now, actually."

"What's going on?" Kevin looked up from the soapy dishwater. "Did you say Morgan's coming? How come nobody told me?" His attention turned at the sound of a motor, and, looking out the kitchen window, he saw a fishing boat dropping anchor at the entrance to the bay. "Whose boat is that?"

"It's Morgan!" Courtney leaped up and ran outside, calling back to the others to hurry.

"What's going on?" Kevin asked again.

"Mr. Nickerson has offered us a trip on the water," his mum said. "Morgan suggested it last night when he brought Courtney home, and phoned this morning to confirm it. Would you like to come? It'll do you good."

"I thought I was grounded."

"You can be grounded with us on the boat," said his dad. "And by the way, I was wrong to assume you'd been drinking last night."

Dad, admitting he was wrong? Kevin almost choked.

"But you did miss your curfew, and your behavior when you came home—well, you know better than that. So you're grounded after the boat ride and all day tomorrow. Got it?"

Kevin nodded. A fair punishment, all things considered, especially if he could use the laptop. Encyclopedia-Titanica had a list of the crew and passengers. Annie McConnell's name could be on it.

Chapter Twenty-Four

Kevin lay in the dark, his eyes wide open in an attempt to stay awake. If he fell asleep and heard the voice one more time, he swore he'd—what? What could he do?

He had hoped that finding Michael's birth certificate would end the ghost's "visitations," but it hadn't. He was still seeing Annie's ghost and hearing her voice and waking everybody up with his shouting. His appointment with the doctor couldn't come soon enough, as far as his parents were concerned. A lot of good that would do.

He thought of the disappointment he'd felt earlier that day when he'd searched through the *Titanic's* passenger list without finding Annie McConnell's name. It didn't mean that she hadn't been on board, not necessarily. He'd read somewhere that the list itself might not have been complete, and that boarding cards hadn't always been a hundred percent accurate. Officials being distracted, or in a hurry to fill things out, or not concentrating. Annie could have showed up at the last minute and been hustled aboard without the proper procedures being followed.

He'd gone from the general passenger list to one that listed the unidentified bodies picked up by the *Mackay-Bennett*. He was scanning the remarks made for each body when he found a description that matched Annie's appearance, both in the photograph and in the way she'd looked to Kevin. He'd copied the remarks, and knew them by heart. Even thinking about them made the back of his neck prickle.

Female, third class, estimated age 17, dark hair, long black overcoat, blue serge jacket and skirt, white blouse, black underdress, woollen combinations, no corsets, black boots and stockings, thin copper wire twisted around ring finger.

Like many of the other descriptions, the remarks ended with the words *No other aids to identification.*

"Right," Kevin said. No other aids, thanks to Angus Seaton. Provided that Kevin's theory was correct and Seaton had taken the purse.

He wondered how the person writing the description knew that she had been a third-class passenger. Maybe from her clothing, or from the fact that she wasn't wearing any jewelry. A twist of copper wire was hardly a diamond ring.

His eyelids were getting heavy. "Stay awake," he said firmly, and laughed. It never made a difference. Except that he somehow felt braver when he was awake.

He could have, should have, gone to the Celtic music concert in Lunenburg with his dad and Courtney. He didn't like all the fiddling and step-dancing, but it would have taken his mind off ghosts and kept him awake longer.

He could wake up his mum and talk to her, but she'd gone to bed early with a migraine and wouldn't want to be disturbed. He could go downstairs, turn on the lights and eat something, read the ghost book again.

It was interesting, the book Mrs. Nickerson had found for him. The idea was that ghosts were the spirits of dead people who couldn't pass from the physical world into the spiritual world because they had some unfinished business. So they were restless, in a sort of limbo, between here and there. Like in Annie's case, needing to find out about Michael.

Kevin figured that she'd tried to find out through Angus Seaton. And when he couldn't or wouldn't help, she'd come to Kevin.

He thought he'd given her what she wanted when he'd found the pictures and birth certificate. But what she wanted was to know what had happened to Michael after the *Titanic* went down....

He wished that he hadn't asked Mrs. Nickerson so many questions, because now he knew too much, like Angus Seaton's going into a mental hospital. Seeing a doctor was one thing, but what if *he* ended up the same way? Zack would go ape, and the kids at school—Kevin would never live it down....

Stay awake! He could turn on the lamp, but that wouldn't keep her away. It would only light up the picture frame and the remains of the box. That was the last thing he wanted to see. He wondered if he could get the box repaired, or repair it himself. A winter project.

Okay, think of projects. School projects. Kevin's had never been the best in the class, but they hadn't been the worst. Average. Not because he lacked creativity. Ha! He was creative—he'd created a ghost, hadn't he?

His laughter was the last thing he heard until the sound of lapping water woke him up, his skin corpse-cold, his sodden sheet wrapped around his body, clammy with the smell of the sea.

He heard a footfall. It couldn't be *her*. Ghosts didn't make footfalls. They glided or floated.

What have you done with my precious boy?

Kevin opened his mouth but could not speak, could scarcely breathe for the tightness in his chest. He threw off the sheet and stepped out of bed, stepped into water, ice water sloshing against his feet, the bed, the walls ... the walls tilting ... the room tilting.

Oh God. This time was different. Something was happening. He had never felt so afraid ... But he was asleep, wasn't he? He'd wake up....

A hand reached out. He stepped back, the water now lapping his knees, and though he did not want to look, he had no choice. He was facing the ghost, her white face framed by wet black hair, her eyes a deep, deep-water blue.

Come, she said. *Help me find Michael.*

Show me what has become of my boy.
Does he walk on land, searching for me?
How will he know me? How will he know me?
You may not sleep, robber of the dead—

"STOP!" Kevin screamed. *"I CAN'T STAND ANY MORE!"*
Throwing on his clothes, he ran blindly out the door and down the stairs.
"No more, no more, I can't stand it!"

"Kevin! Honey, stop! What are you doing?"

"Go away, you freak! You go and find Michael, he's nothing to me—"

"Kevin, it's Mum—"

"Don't touch me!" He pushed her hand away, and tore out of the house
and down to the beach, looking over his shoulder to see if she was following. Yes, oh God, yes, she was coming down the verandah steps, onto the
beach, after him. "Stay away from me!"

The dory wouldn't do, not now, no way was he rowing out like Angus
Seaton and ending up drowned. Now he needed speed.

Into the dinghy, push off from shore, full throttle out of the bay and over
an invisible line to open water. A starry night, no moon, a glistening wake
cutting into the inky black of the sea, white sea froth marking the curve of
Shearwater Bay and the long stretch of Plover Beach, receding like the
pinpricks of light from shore.

"I'm invincible," Kevin shouted, exhilarated by the rush of being out
on the water alone. "*Crazy* invincible, Annie McConnell, you *goth freak*.
Where's Michael? Who the hell cares? Get over it, it's over, you're dead,
you're both dead!"

The rush, the power! He would shout and laugh, and if he saw her on
the water he would blast through her until she was ghost-dead-gone and
gone for good.

He swung the boat wide in a circle, doubling back to cross over the
wake, drawing lines and spirals of silver. "See that, Annie? I'm here!"
Riding over the waves, rising high and hitting down hard with a thumping *thwack.* "Hear that, Annie?" *Thwack.* Vibrations jolting his body, his
hand shaking on the throttle, he had the whole ocean to himself.

Where was he now? He'd lost sight of the shore, had no idea how far he'd gone. The hazy cluster in the distance...a town or a lighthouse? Halifax? A group of ghosts? He laughed, loon-like. "A moaning of ghosts? A spook—" Without warning, the engine sputtered and died. "No way!" he raged. He fiddled with the choke and pulled the starter cord. Tried and tried again, ignoring the voice in his head, his father saying, "You're flooding it, you idiot. Don't you know anything? Hopeless, hopeless..."

Kevin knew he was flooding it, but he couldn't wait, he had to keep moving because Annie McConnell had never appeared when he was moving fast, and he had to keep moving because the waves were getting bigger and rocking the boat, breaking over the bow and the sides.

He stood up and yanked the starter cord. Nothing.

He pulled a second time, fighting to keep his balance, knowing that standing in a boat was an insane thing to do, but he was crazy anyway so what difference did it make and what else could he do?

A promising *click*. "Yes," Kevin cried triumphantly. "One more go and we've got it." He was adjusting his stance to steady himself when a wave caught him unawares, flipped the boat, and trapped him underneath.

He swam deeper and off to the side, trying to judge the distance. Too far and he'd be away from the boat, not far enough and he'd still be underneath. He broke the surface gasping and sputtering, saw the boat and managed to reach it in a few hard strokes.

Wasted. Exhilaration, energy, gone. His hands gripped the gunnel, but he couldn't stay like that. Somehow he had to get out of the water.

His dad would love this scenario. *You stupid kid, going off without a life jacket. Don't you know anything? What were you thinking? How many times have I told you?*

Angered by the voice in his head, Kevin summoned the strength to pull his upper body over the hull. Waves breaking over his head, and the boat drifting to God only knew where.

When had it become so cold?

Pans of ice drifted by on the current. An iceberg loomed on the horizon.

Kevin's lungs burned with cold. Every breath was a struggle. His eye-lashes prickled with frost; his eyes were stinging with salt and tears.

Tremors shuddered through his body. He wanted to let go and sink into sleep, wanted nothing more than the relief of closing his eyes and falling, falling into a deep sleep, but he knew—the one thing he knew—that he had to stay awake.

Something on the sea was changing. An upheaval of water, a surge, a swell of waves—and the stern of a ship emerged: the stern, the amidships, all the way along to the bow. The ship blazed against the blackness of sky and water, glowed and sparkled with light, pulsed with the thrum of engines, the sounds of music and laughter, and ahead in its path, unno-ticed, loomed the dark mountainous shape of the iceberg.

The sea had calmed. Looking over the glassy stillness, Kevin saw a pale light moving toward him, a light taking shape before his eyes, emerg-ing as the ghost of Annie McConnell.

"Let go," she said. *"Follow me."*

He let go willingly and slipped away. His body weightless, floating toward the light, wondering, Is this what it's like to die...am I already dead...who do you think you are...you used to be...somebody...

Thoughts skipping like stones across a mirrored sea, skipping toward a horizon and gone.

Chapter Twenty-Five

April 14, 1912, 11:40 P.M.

At the moment of letting go, Kevin felt strangely calm. It was a relief to follow the ghost, to slip away into a sea of surprising warmth and light and forgetfulness.

A sudden shaking and the sound of scraping metal jolted him to his senses. With electrifying clarity, he knew that he was on the *Titanic*.

The shock propelled him to his feet. There was no sign of Annie. He'd followed her, but she'd disappeared. Left him lying facedown on deck at the moment the ship hit the iceberg.

He had to find her. Had to find the third-class quarters, find her cabin and get her and Michael to a lifeboat. But first he had to get his bearings.

He was on the well deck at the bow end, that much he knew because he could see the crow's nest on the forward mast. Ice shaved off by the collision littered the deck. Close by, a group of young men were kicking a chunk of ice around in a makeshift game of soccer, marveling about the near miss. To have come so close and not hit the iceberg head-on? A miracle. No wonder they were in high spirits.

They didn't know that the pressure of the ice against the hull had caused the steel plates to buckle and the rivets to pop. They didn't know that the sea, at that very second, was flowing in. They didn't know that in less than three hours the unthinkable would have happened. How could they know? Kevin was the only one on board who knew.

He cried out to the men, "Get your life belts!"

They looked up from their game and laughed.

Kevin wasn't surprised. If he could see himself through their eyes, he'd laugh, too—a gangly kid in shorts and a hoodie, popping up from nowhere and acting like a captain. "It's true," he insisted. "We're sinking."

"Sinking? This ship's unsinkable," one of the men said.

Others joined in the ribbing.

"What'll your mum think? A boy like you, still in short pants, passed out on deck. Shameful."

"Get your stockings on before your knees turn blue."

"Best get below and sleep it off. Hey, lads! Back to the game."

"Wait!" Kevin called out. "Where's my cabin? I—I've forgotten the number."

"Not up here. The bow end's only for single men. You're with your parents?"

Kevin nodded. A lie made more sense than the truth.

"You'll be at the stern. E deck, F, G—one of the decks below. Once you're inside, go down the stairs to E deck and follow Scotland Road. That'll take you to the end of the ship." He snorted. "If she don't sink first!"

Kevin gave a wry laugh. Yeah, funny. He thanked them and wished them luck.

The warmth of the interior hit him like a sauna. He hadn't realized how cold he was, and the thought of going back outside and getting into an open lifeboat—but he couldn't think about that now.

C deck. Down two flights of stairs to E deck and he was on Scotland Road. A connector route, a passageway running the length of the ship. He had to move quickly.

The book he'd read at school, the one called *882 ½ Amazing Answers to Your Questions about the* Titanic—he'd wondered about the title, and found out it was the length of the ship, 882.5 feet. As long as twenty school buses parked end to end.

Too bad he hadn't memorized the book, or a set of deck plans, so he could find his way around, because getting Annie and Michael to the boat deck where the lifeboats were stored was going to be crazy once the rest of the passengers started to move. They'd be heading for the stern, the part of the ship that would rise as the forward compartments filled with water and dragged the bow down. The part of the ship that would draw throngs of people because they would think it was the safest place to be, the place where they could wait until they were rescued.

How much farther did he have to go on Scotland Road? He was checking the signs as he passed by, watching for third-class areas, sleeping quarters, staircases, exits. There was no one around to ask. After midnight, the passageway was empty. Had he covered the length of ten buses or only five? How far along would he have to go? Would he find Annie on E deck? Why had she left him? If she wanted his help . . .

The answer hit with the force of a Taser. She wasn't a ghost on the ship. She was a living person. She didn't want his help, not now. She didn't need it. Her baby was safe. As far as Annie knew, she was on her way to New York to start a new life. She didn't know what was coming. She didn't know Kevin . . . and how was he going to handle that? He had to come up with a story, something that would convince her to trust him. If he pretended he had known her in Belfast . . .

He was passing through a section of crew's quarters when an idea came to him. Before he could think it through, the ship began to vibrate, shaking and rattling with such force he had to stop and grab the handrail to keep his balance. He knew what that meant. One by one the engines were being shut down, the steady, reassuring thrum replaced by silence.

The noisy vibrations followed by the eerie, unfamiliar silence were enough to awaken all but the strongest sleepers. If Kevin didn't find Annie soon, the stairs and passageways would be dangerously crowded, if not impassable.

He hurried through the crew's quarters, stepping aside as crewmen emerged from their cabins, buttoning their jackets as they rushed for the stairs.

He pushed on to a third-class section where passengers were milling in the passageway, asking questions in English and in languages that Kevin didn't know. "What happened? Do you know? Does anybody know? Did we hit something? Why have the engines stopped?"

A steward was telling people to get their life belts—but only as a precaution, there was no need to worry—and to stay in their cabins until further notice.

"Annie McConnell!" Kevin yelled in passing. "Anybody here know Annie?"

No answer.

Down another level to F deck and more third-class sleeping quarters.

Kevin tried again. "Annie! Annie McConnell!"

More people in the passageway. Men and women, half-dressed, fully dressed, in pajamas or robes, children half-asleep and tearful, everyone confused, fearful, anxious, curious, but not panicking, not yet, because the stern was too far from the bow, they wouldn't have felt the collision...but did they notice that the ship was tilting? Only a little, but enough to know that the bow was starting to nose down and the stern was beginning to rise. Kevin had to wonder how much longer he had. Even if he didn't find Annie, he had to get to a lifeboat himself to survive.

"Is something wrong? Did we hit something? Are we in any danger? What should we do?"

"Nothing's wrong.... I heard she hit an iceberg.... She's unsinkable.... Go back to sleep...."

Passengers milling around, looking for relatives, asking questions, trying to answer, guessing, wondering, thinking out loud. "Should we go back to sleep? Should we go out on deck?" Wondering if they should go to the men's quarters to find other family members, or if they should wait for the men to come to them. Wondering if they should stay where they were and wait for the engines to start up again, wondering where was the steward to tell them what to do, where was an officer, wasn't there anyone who knew what was going on?

Passengers curious and excited, rushing for the stairs to go out on deck and see for themselves. "Icebergs? How thrilling! Were you out on deck? Did you see the iceberg? How big? How high? How long will it take it to melt? Did it cause much damage? Shall we go have a look?"

"Annie! Anyone know Annie McConnell?"

Kevin was expecting more blank looks when two women paused on their way to the stairs. "You mean the girl with wee Michael?" the younger one said. "She's on G deck, directly below, but I couldn't tell you the cabin number. We sit together for meals. Wait!" she said, as Kevin turned to rush off. "Do you know what's happening?"

He looked over his shoulder and told them they were sinking. Heard their laughter as they climbed up the stairs.

G deck. His last chance to find Annie.

He pounded on cabin doors, calling her name. Every second now could be a second too late. Too late for the boat deck, too late for the lifeboats, and here he was, nearing the extreme end of the stern and still no luck.

Suddenly he stopped. Made a complete turn and went back to the half-open cabin door where he'd caught a glimpse of a girl who could, possibly, be her—a dark-haired girl in a black nightgown or something, sitting on a berth playing pat-a-cake with a baby. "Annie McConnell!" He burst inside. "Are you Annie?"

He looked down at her hand. It was her, all right. He knew by the copper-wire ring on her finger.

Chapter Twenty-Six

"Stop right this minute!" Annie put down the baby, leaped to her feet, and glared at Kevin, her dark blue eyes almost black with fury.

"How do you know my name? Did John's father send you, to make sure I got away?"

"No, you've got it wrong—"

"Oh, isn't that so like Lord Muck. It wasn't enough to return the photographs—they weren't even his—and it wasn't enough to send us away, me and Michael—not even a first-class ticket, him with his filthy wealth, but oh no, wouldn't waste money on a factory girl and her baby—"

"Stop!" Kevin was stunned. "For God's sake!" The girl was so different from what he'd been expecting—and she was still going on.

"—and Michael being his own grandson, that he and his missus offered to raise as their own in exchange for money! Am I that desperate, I'd sell my child? And then he sends a lackey like you—"

"*John* sent me!" Kevin blurted.

"What?" She gaped at Kevin, clearly taken aback. "John Collins?"

Kevin nodded, relieved beyond belief that he'd gotten the name right. "He sent me to make sure you and Michael were all right."

"How do you know—?"

"There's no time to explain," Kevin said. "Put on warm clothes, same for Michael, and hurry. We're going out on deck." He spotted the life belts on top of the wardrobe and pulled them down. "Don't just stand there! The ship's hit an iceberg and we're sinking." Was that his voice? His manner and words astounded him, as if someone else had replaced the Kevin he knew.

Annie's two cabin-mates had opened their privacy curtains and were leaning over their upper berths. The red-haired woman gave Kevin a worried look. "Sinking? Do you know that for a fact?"

The woman opposite snorted. "How could he know, for all his big talk? Look at him, still wet behind the ears, acting the captain."

"He's leaving." Annie shoved Kevin hard in the chest. "Out, you daft beggar. I don't believe a word you're saying."

"You think I'm joking? Put on some warm clothes."

She held her ground, her face a murderous scowl. "Not until you tell me about John—"

"There's no time." Kevin pushed past and opened the valise at the foot of Annie's bunk. He rummaged quickly through the clothing—some hers, some Michael's—tossing out a warm-looking skirt and jacket, a blouse and some woollen under-stuff he didn't want to think about. "Put this on over top of that thing you're wearing. I'll get Michael ready myself."

Michael began to wail, his small fists clenched, his face scrunched up like a wrinkled tomato. "Hey, little guy," Kevin said, struggling to put knitted bootees on the baby's feet. Underneath the long flannel nightgown his legs kicked out with surprising strength.

"You want to get going, don't you, Michael? Just like your dad," Kevin said. Guessing wildly, hoping it didn't sound too far-fetched, he added, "I was a stable hand, looked after John's horse, and when he heard I was planning to go to America, he bought me a ticket on the *Titanic* so I could keep an eye out for you and your mother. He knew he could trust me."

Glancing over his shoulder, Kevin saw that Annie was listening and, what's more, she was starting to do what he'd asked. "Haven't you got anything warmer?" he said. "Socks, boots, mittens—winter stuff, like thermals and fleece?"

"Oh, so I'm a sheep now? Who are you? Do you have a name?"

"Get Michael to stop crying. Sing or something."

"Do you hear that, Michael, love?" Her voice softened. "We'd like to know who he thinks he is, Lord Bossy Boots, the stable hand."

Michael looked up and laughed.

"That's better, my darlin'. We'll humor Lord Bossy Boots, shall we? We'll all be keeping calm now." She fired a look at Kevin.

Like it's my fault? He fired the look straight back. She was right, though. He had to calm down. Outside the cabin, passengers were looking in and asking what was going on, why was the lad in such a panic, had he heard something?

Ignoring them, Kevin concentrated on bundling Michael in flannel vests and woollen sweaters, a knitted cap, and bootees for his hands. "Six little slits in the hull, each as wide as a man's finger. Okay, Michael? That's what the iceberg did. Right up at that bow. Punch, punch, punch...the metal plates buckle, the rivets pop. Six little slits, that's all..." He spoke softly as he was dressing Michael, more to calm himself than the baby, and found that his voice had a soothing effect. "See, Michael, it wasn't what people thought at first. The iceberg didn't cut a gash in the side the way a can opener slices a tin can. If it had been like that, the ship would sink fast. But with six little slits, the water doesn't come in all at the same time. So everybody has a chance to get to the boat deck and into a lifeboat."

"What are you talking about?" Annie railed. "What language is it you're speaking? It's not like any English I've ever heard."

"Thing is," Kevin went on, talking to Michael but saying it for Annie, "you have to believe it. If you stay down here because you believe the *Titanic*'s unsinkable, well, it's game over. Is your mum listening, Michael? We're going to the boat deck. That's why you look like a little doughboy. But we're not through yet."

He wrapped Michael snugly in one of the two shawls lying on Annie's berth, then picked up the life belt. It was more like a vest, with four ties on each side. It was heavy, bulky, and huge on a baby, but if *he* were to wear it, with Michael tucked inside and securely strapped to his body, it would work.

"Now what are you doing?" Annie demanded, attempting to shove him aside. "If there's any carrying to be done, I'll do it."

"Get back!" Kevin said. "John Collins trusted me, why can't you? This is the best way to keep Michael safe. And just so you know, John was pleased that you crossed out 'unknown' and wrote his name on the birth certificate."

"He told you that, a stable boy?"

Kevin swore under his breath. Bad move, bringing that up. Ignoring her question, he took the second shawl and made a baby sling, arranging the ends to cross behind his back and tie at his waist. "See what I'm doing, Michael? This is in case my belt gets loose, so you won't slide down. Cool, eh? You're like a baby kangaroo." He looked up at Annie. "What do you think? Now I put the life belt on...and Michael's wrapped up snug. He can even keep an eye on you." Kevin smiled. "He won't even need all this once you're in the lifeboat, but if we don't get—"

"He won't be needing it at all!" Annie said, moving in to release her baby.

"You can't!" Kevin held up a hand to stop her. "It's a nightmare getting up there. I've seen the movie—the stairs and passageways and crowds, and the water coming in and the boat at an angle—"

"Movie? What are you saying now? Who *are* you?"

"Can you feel how the ship's tilting? Every second it's a bit more. If my hands are free I can help you, and I'll give Michael to you as soon as we get to the lifeboats. Now put your life belt on—"

"Wait! Not without my pictures."

"You don't need..." He stopped, realizing what she meant.

She took the miniature picture frame from a box beneath her berth and placed it inside a small leather purse. "To keep it dry," she said. "Not that I believe a word you're saying. Sinking? John Collins and a stable boy? It's laughable."

Kevin watched as she put the purse in her coat pocket. A long, black overcoat with at least a dozen buttons... "Never mind that," he said sharply, turning from the sight of her fingers fumbling at the buttons. "Just your life belt. We're going."

They'd no sooner stepped into the passageway than a steward came by. "There's no cause to worry," he was saying. "Everyone, please wait in your cabins for official instructions."

"So, Lord Bossy." Annie stamped her foot. "Didn't we tell you? All this to-do for nothing."

Her cabin mates, who had started to put on warm clothing, decided to stay put and advised Annie to do the same.

"A grand idea," she said. "Do you hear that, Michael? Let's—You! Stop right there!"

"Follow me," Kevin shouted. He was running across the passageway to the stairs, knowing she'd catch up as long as he had Michael.

He felt a tug on his hoodie but kept going, saying over his shoulder, "You'd believe me if your cabin was at the bow end. Know why? 'Cause it'd be flooded. That's right, the bow's already going down. Why would I make this up? How stupid do you think I am?"

"Who are you? How do you know these things?"

"Doesn't matter," he said. "You have to trust me the way John Collins trusted me. If you're still not sure about that, how else would I know that Michael was born on July 11, 1911?" Seven-eleven—thank God it was an easy date to remember.

She had to be shocked by that bit of information. Shocked into silence, judging from the lack of a comeback.

The stairs took them to E deck, where Scotland Road had become a stream of desperate passengers making for the stern.

"Hold on to me," Kevin ordered. "Don't let go. Understand?"

"We must be going the wrong way!" she argued. "Why's everyone going in the opposite direction? We've got to turn..."

Kevin stopped listening. In one of the third-class passageways leading off Scotland Road, a steward, unlike the one on G deck, was ordering women and children to go to the boat deck. Children were crying, women were refusing to leave without their husbands—scenes of anxiety and confusion like the ones he had seen earlier, now heightened by panic and terror.

Stairs . . . where was the next set of stairs? Kevin fought against the flow, trusting that Annie wouldn't risk letting go and being swept away. Hundreds of men were coming from the third-class forward quarters, carrying belongings, dragging valises, many speaking in foreign languages. Kevin had no doubt that some were fathers and older brothers going to the aft quarters to find wives, daughters, sisters, and friends.

At one point the crush was so heavy he and Annie could move only by flattening themselves against the wall and edging sideways. A man whom Kevin recognized as one of the soccer players paused long enough to say, "Sorry I doubted you, lad. Our room's underwater. Shoes, coat, everything's afloat."

"Go to the boat deck, not the stern," Kevin called after him, thinking that if he himself didn't know any better, he'd probably go to the stern. Because wouldn't you want to be as far from the sinking bow as you could get? Wouldn't you think that the ship might level off and stay afloat until another ship came to your rescue? Wouldn't you keep hoping, hoping—

How far along was the next staircase? Would they make it in time? He was beginning to despair when he saw an open door that connected Scotland Road to a staircase. "Quick, Annie, in here."

"We can't! See the sign? It's second class."

"What can they do? Throw us overboard? Come on!"

Second class, first class, he didn't care. All he could think about was the boat deck. Lifeboats being loaded, passengers lowered to safety.

He heard someone call out the time. 1:20 A.M. They were running out of time.

The next several minutes passed in a terrifying confusion of doors, stairs, passageways, sounds, and images.

D deck awash with seawater, sloshing against walls and up to their knees, littered with floating debris . . .

Playing cards, a doll with a smiling face...

A cry of alarm, Annie tripping over an abandoned valise...

People running, their feet making a pattering sound...

Ropes of jewelry hanging from a woman's neck...

The ship tilting more and more and more... steep uphill climbs toward the stern, dangerous downward slopes to the bow... brace yourself, Annie, hang on to the rail, don't fall, please God please God...

Water, water, everywhere—Stop. He couldn't think of that.

A blur of passengers, scared, excited, annoyed, confused, anxious, terrified, panicking, stammering, sobbing, crying, arguing, shouting, agonizing over what to do.... Go or stay? Which way? Which door? Which staircase? Where are the life belts? What should we take? "Good-bye, see you later," a father saying to his son.

See you later. Words that Kevin had spoken a million times, never thinking that there might not be a later.

Michael sound asleep, unaware of the chaos around him.

A door marked *Exit to Promenade*... locked. Dead end. Oh, God. No, no, no.... Pulse thudding, throat strangling, stomach sick with the rush of adrenaline, turning to go back and the door opening. First-class steward. "Boat deck? Follow me."

A miracle. Thank you, God.

A winding course through elegant rooms and passageways to another door. *Exit to Boat Deck.*

Kevin shook the steward's hand. "Thank you. And good luck," he said, his voice close to breaking.

Chapter Twenty-Seven

The cold bit into his lungs. Each breath came out as a gasping cough, and for a moment he couldn't speak. Not that he would have been heard. The noise was deafening. Creaking block and tackle, shrieks of steam bursting out of the funnels, passengers from all three classes facing the fact that the *Titanic* was sinking, and sinking fast, passengers delirious, calm, hysterical, dazed, stunned, shocked.

Kevin was beyond shock. The ship's bow was underwater. The deck was sloping sharply. The lifeboats were gone. No, there was a boat being loaded. Not a regular lifeboat, but one of the collapsibles with canvas sides. "We made it, Annie. They're loading a lifeboat—*Annie!*"

Where had she gone? She should have been right behind him. Sick with panic, he craned his neck to spot her. Where, where—there. Off to the side, cut off by a throng of frantic men.

"*Annie!*" He caught her eye, placed a protective hand over Michael's head and moved toward her, using elbows, shoulders, whatever it took to squeeze a way through the crowd.

"Women and children!" an officer was shouting. "Any more women and children?"

"Yes!" Kevin cried. "Wait!"

"*You've* no hope of getting on." A man standing in Kevin's way gave him an angry look. "Didn't you hear the officer? *Children* first."

"I've got a baby, let me pass!" Kevin shot back, showing him Michael. Surprised, the man stepped aside.

Kevin didn't understand. Why didn't the man think he was a child? That's what the men playing soccer had thought, and the women in Annie's cabin. But that felt like years ago...

The men were moving aside to let women and children reach the lifeboat, and seeing that Kevin was carrying a baby, they did the same for him.

Now he could move more quickly. Michael had woken and was squirming around with such strength Kevin had to hold him in place with both hands for fear he'd slip out of the makeshift pack. He'd be crying soon, if Kevin didn't reach Annie. Where had she gone now? He'd lost sight of her for two seconds, but in that time the crowd had shifted and taller, burlier men had cut her off from his view.

"Michael!" Her voice rang out. "I'm here, Michael!"

Hearing his mother, Michael started to howl.

Kevin spotted her up ahead. "I've got him, we're coming," he hollered, and started to push his way through.

The closer he got to her and the lifeboat, the more difficult it became. Women crying hysterically, refusing to get into the lifeboat without their husbands; children crying as they said good-bye to their fathers; fathers promising they'd get into another lifeboat and find them.

He caught another sight of Annie. He was raising his arm to wave, certain he'd reach her in time, when a man in a dinner jacket lifted her off her feet and carried her to the rail.

"Put me down!" She was yelling, kicking, smacking the man's back. "Michael, my baby! Put me down!"

"Let me through!" Kevin shouted. The man had put Annie into the lifeboat. If she didn't do anything foolish, like climbing back onto the ship to get Michael, she'd be safe. Kevin would reach the lifeboat in time and he and Michael would be safe.

He was almost to the rail when he found that his way was blocked by a pack of male passengers trying to storm the lifeboat. A line of crewmen, standing with their arms interlocked, were trying to hold them back. Both sides were desperate, struggling and pushing against the other, until an officer drew out his revolver, raised it in the air, and fired a shot.

The men froze.

"Women and children only!" the officer commanded. "Men must stay behind. Lower the boat."

"Wait!" Kevin cried. "The baby!" He fumbled with the belt and straps, frozen fingers uselessly working the double and triple knots that bound Michael to him and, at the same time, fighting to get to the lifeboat. "A knife, I need a knife, I've got to cut this—please, somebody—"

"Too late, son," a crewman said kindly. "The boat's in the water—"

"It can't be! The baby's mother—"

"You'll have to wait for another."

Kevin wanted to cry. He wanted his own mother to be there, to tell him that everything would be fine. He wanted his father to be there, to tell him—what? The usual, that he was reckless and stupid? Couldn't his father tell him, for once, that he was brave, that he'd tried, that he'd done his best?

There was one boat left on the port side, a collapsible stowed above the deck, on the roof of the officers' quarters. The crew hadn't even gotten it down yet. One boat on the port side, possibly another on the starboard side, and hundreds of people on deck, at the stern, or down below. Kevin pushed the thought from his mind.

"We'll make it, Michael," he said, stroking the baby's head. "We'll catch up to your mum, you'll see." Michael hadn't settled down, but at the sound of Kevin's voice he stopped fussing and smiled. It gave Kevin courage, but he couldn't smile back. His heart had lodged in the pit of his stomach. His emotions were spent.

The crew was struggling to launch the collapsible, propping up oars to serve as a ramp. But as the boat began to slide down, the oars smashed beneath its weight. The boat rolled over and landed in the water upside down.

Howling with despair, the crowd rushed to the remaining collapsible on the starboard side, their one last hope.

Kevin fought against the surge. There wasn't time to get to the starboard side, and, given the crowd, the chances of getting a place on the boat—if it hadn't already left—were slim. The ship was going down even faster. The drop to the water was less than ten feet now. Kevin knew he could dive off or jump, but that wasn't safe, not with the baby, not with the amount of debris in the water.

A rope. His hands were free, he could shimmy down one of the ropes hanging from the davits. Annie would see him and see that he had Michael. She'd get the oarsmen on her boat to go back for them.

He seized the closest rope, wrapped his legs around it, and began to lower himself. "Here we go, Michael. Your mum will see us and everything will be okay."

He had no sooner spoken than the bow of the *Titanic* made its final plunge.

Chapter Twenty-Eight

A giant wave swept up the deck, tore the rope from Kevin's hands, and washed everyone into the sea.

He treaded water, fighting to keep Michael's head above the waves. He saw people swimming toward the overturned collapsible, saw that people were already on it, and made for it himself, using every stroke he knew to keep the baby's head out of the water, praying he'd reach the boat before hypothermia—

A screeching tear of metal caused him to look up. The forward funnel of the *Titanic* was falling over, crashing into the sea in an explosion of sparks and soot, crushing everyone directly below.

The wave created by the crash knocked Kevin under. He came up in an instant, spluttering and gasping, with Michael coughing up seawater and wailing.

He scanned the sea, looking for the overturned lifeboat, and saw that it had been swept away and out of reach. The people who'd been standing on it were gone.

Keep moving, Kevin told himself. Tread water. Rub your hands together, rub them on Michael's head, because their body heat was all they had and it was going fast. Below-zero water was seeping through their clothing, their skin, their bones. Ten minutes before hypothermia set in . . . depending on what? Your age? Your weight? If he were fat he'd have a better chance. It came into his mind from somewhere that one of the ship's cooks was fat and survived. He'd started drinking whiskey when he knew the ship was doomed, got thrown over by the wave, and survived in the water for two hours.

Just then Kevin heard someone call out, "Take the oar!" Turning his head, he saw a half-empty lifeboat coming toward him. A lady was holding out an oar, urging him to take hold. He fought to unlock his fingers and forced his hands to clasp the oar, praying that they would not give out on him.

Two men leaned over and lifted him aboard, bursting out with excitement when they saw the baby tucked inside Kevin's life belt.

"You're safe and the baby's safe," said the lady who'd held out the oar. She took the knife offered by a fellow passenger and cut the straps of Michael's makeshift pouch, removed his clothing, and wrapped him in a dry blanket. That done, she began rubbing his arms and legs and chest to get some warmth back into him. "You need to do the same," she said to Kevin.

Kevin reached out his arms. "Give . . ." His mouth couldn't form the words. He wanted to tell her that Michael was his responsibility.

"You look after yourself first," said another woman on board. She handed Kevin a blanket. "Rub your hands, move your arms—the baby's coming 'round already, the brave little soul. What's his name?"

"Michael." He draped the blanket over his shoulders and hugged it to his chest. It didn't make much difference. Rowing would warm him up. The men at the oars were looking tired but they didn't dare stop to rest, not with the ship going down, and with the amount of debris in the water their progress was slow. The rowers in the other lifeboats were doing the same. Because when the ship went down, they thought, they'd be drawn down by the suction.

Kevin wanted to tell them not to worry. There would be no suction. But was that really the way it was? He wasn't sure anymore, what was real and what wasn't.

The sounds were real. Every human sound of pain, fear, terror, loss. *It was sad, so sad, it was sad, so sad...husbands and wives, little children lost their lives...* How could he have sung that song and made a joke of it? It must have been somebody else.

Where was Annie? She was put into a lifeboat...or was it a collapsible? Was it the one that overturned? He couldn't remember. Was she one of the people struggling in the water, crying out for help? They were alive, but no one in a lifeboat would pick them up.

"Why can't we go back for them?" a little girl in the lifeboat was asking her mother.

"Because there are too many, dearest. They'd swamp our boat and we would all be lost. Do you see? I know it's not fair."

"We picked him up with the baby," she said, glancing over at Kevin.

"That's because he was apart from the others, and not far from our lifeboat. Come, dearest." She drew her daughter close and covered her ears to shut out the sound of wailing voices.

The ship still blazed with light, from the waterline to the stern. In every cabin on every deck and up to the masthead, the lights were on. The band was still playing. Not lively tunes, but hymns.

"Let me," Kevin said, indicating to the rower that he would take a turn at the oars. Anything to keep his mind off the cries for help, and the movement would help keep him warm.

The man nodded gratefully. But as Kevin was moving to take the man's place, he heard Annie.

"Michael!" Her voice was a haunting, keening wail, rising through and above all other sounds.

Kevin desperately searched the water. Where was she? There, in the collapsible. He grabbed Michael from the lady's arms, telling her it was Annie, Michael's mother, in the collapsible. He held Michael high so

Annie could see he was safe. She raised her hands, palms pressed together as if in a prayer of thanks. Thanks to God...or to Kevin? The important thing was that she knew her baby would survive.

He hugged Michael and, knowing that the baby would stay warmer with the lady, handed him back.

"There, there," she murmured, tucking him inside her fur coat. "Your mama knows you're safe, little Michael, and isn't that a blessing." Her voice caught, and she wiped her eyes. "To be separated from someone, to have someone left behind..."

"Did you...." The woman next to her spoke gently.

"No, thank the Lord. My fiancé is meeting me in New York. We're to be married..."

Kevin paid little attention to the talk that followed. He really had to get up and row for a while, since he'd offered—"What?" he blurted, his head jerking up. He fixed his gaze on the lady with Michael. "What did you just say?"

She gave a startled smile. "Miss Margaret Dyson. My name."

"No, *before* that."

"Messenger and Ross, the accounting firm. I was saying that George Messenger's my fiancé."

He *had* heard her correctly. *Messenger*...But before he could say more, he saw to his horror that Annie was out of the boat and swimming toward them.

God! Of all the insane—to be so desperate to reach Michael that she'd do something so stupid? How could she? Why? Didn't she know they were safe, that the rescue ship was on its way?

"Annie, no!" he screamed. He wanted to tell her to get back to the collapsible. She'd never make it. But she *could*. She wasn't that far away. Unless the cold was too much, unless a wave washed her under, unless, unless...

He had to make sure. He put the life belt back on and dived in before anyone in the boat could stop him. Swam toward her, his eyes focused on the white of her life belt. The water was littered with stuff that people had thrown overboard to use as rafts. He could cling to a door or something if he got tired. So could Annie. He heard the splash of oars as the rowers in his boat came after him, the passengers shouting at him to hold steady, they'd get him and the girl on board.

He had almost reached Annie. He could almost believe she was smiling when a deafening, shuddering, end-of-the-world roar drew their attention away.

Kevin stared. The stern of the *Titanic* was rising. Everything on board that could move was breaking and crashing forward, but the lights stayed on. Half the ship was underwater and the lights were on and the forward half was sinking even deeper.

He continued to stare, horrified yet fascinated, unable to look away. The stern kept rising, rising, until the ship was almost standing. For a moment she hung there, her lights still shining, until suddenly the lights went out.

With the darkness came a shattering sound and an explosion of sparks. Engines, boilers, machinery breaking loose from bolts and mountings, smashing through the ship, tearing her apart. And above that the wrenching sounds of all those left behind, those who had fled to the stern now falling, jumping, clinging to wreckage, thrashing about in the water.

The stern slipped into the sea and the ship was gone. She went down silently, with hardly a ripple.

The cries of those in the water faded until they were gone.

The lights were gone, except for the starlight. And the bluish-white gleam of an iceberg.

Chapter Twenty-Nine

The light was intense.

Rose orange red gold shimmered over the sea and the drifting ice, over flocks of gulls, white gulls rising and falling with the rise and fall of the waves.

Kevin looked again. Not gulls, but life belts holding bodies afloat. Hundreds of bodies. Bodies, bodies everywhere.

Among them, Annie McConnell.

Lifeboats huddled alongside a ship, rope ladders swung over her rail. The *Carpathia* had arrived.

Kevin had been left behind, sprawled over something hard. A door, an overturned boat? His mind had shut down. He was numb, though his eyes were clear. Clear and sharp enough to see the white canvas mailbag coming down the side of the *Carpathia*. He was closer than he'd thought at first—maybe he was drifting toward the ship—because he was close enough to see the lady in the fur coat, Margaret Dyson, putting a baby inside the mailbag. He watched it being hauled up the side of the ship and lifted gently over the rail. Michael McConnell, safely delivered.

He's safe, Annie. Kevin couldn't speak, but the words formed in his mind.

Michael's safe, he survived. You saw him in the lifeboat, you know he's been rescued. He'll know you because I do. He's not lost. You're not forgotten.

Margaret Dyson. Soon to become Mrs. George Messenger. She and her new husband would take care of Michael. That was how it must have happened.

If he were on the *Carpathia* he could tell her that he was a Messenger. He couldn't lift his arm but his mind willed it to wave, to call out to the ship, I'm here, I'm alive, don't leave me. . . .

It was a struggle to hold on. He longed to let go and slip away as he had before. He remembered the calmness, the relief. But if he let go this time, he wouldn't wake up on the *Titanic*. This time . . .

Was that Annie reaching out to him? Floating among the gulls, adrift in the ice? Was she coming for him?

There was something he wanted to tell her, but she was caught in the current and drifting away. He let go and followed, hoping to catch up before she was lost, hoping he'd remember what it was he wanted to say.

The colors of the sunrise were changing, sharpening into one yellow beam, blinding him. The *Carpathia* was gone. The white gulls remained.

"Kevin . . . are you awake?" A girl's voice. Was it Annie?

No need for her to ask *Where's Michael?* She knew. But Kevin wanted to tell her anyway.

He's safe, Annie. You saw him in the lifeboat. You were swimming toward him. Your lips were moving. Were you saying good-bye? Because you can go now, Annie. Michael is not lost. Michael is here. Michael has always been here.

"Kevin, it's Dad."

Another voice.

"You're in the hospital but you're fine. Mum and Courtney are here. We've been so worried."

Kevin moaned. Hospital? He didn't want to be there. He wanted to go back to the other place. He couldn't remember where it was, only that it was silent and deep and full of light.

"What happened, son? Do you remember anything at all?"

"Leave him be, Jim. He's still asleep, he'll wake up when he's ready."

"The doctor said we should talk to him anyway."

"*Talk*, Dad. Not ask questions."

Say something, Kevin told himself. Then they'll leave and you can slip away like before.

He opened his eyes. They were sitting on either side of his hospital bed, their faces creased with concern. He gave a small smile. "The sun was coming up."

His father frowned.

"Sorry," Kevin said, even though he wasn't. It was force of habit. He'd spoken the truth about the sun, whether Dad liked it or not. "The sun was coming up and it was so bright it hurt my eyes. The rest of me was freezing. Do I have frostbite?"

"Kevin, you were picked up in the middle of the night, not at sunrise," his dad said. "The light you thought was the sun must have been from the coast guard vessel."

"Coast guard? Were they picking up the dead bodies? They must have been surprised when I wasn't dead."

His dad's frown deepened. His mother gasped, her eyes wide.

Courtney got up and cranked his bed to a sitting position. Probably to avoid looking at him, probably thinking *Is Kevin kidding? He has to be kidding.* Not knowing whether she should laugh or cry.

"Don't worry, guys," he said. "I know I've got frostbite." He moved the sheet aside to look at his toes, each one individually wrapped in gauze. "I guess they'll have to come off." He paused. "Will my feet have to come off? There was a guy on the *Titanic*, he got his feet amputated, he was in the water so long." Another pause. "Sorry, Dad. I won't be able to play soccer. Good excuse, huh? But I can still swim." His throat was tight.

The next thing he knew, his voice was choking with sobs, his body was shaking, and he hated himself for being such a baby, for not being able to stop. "I thought...I thought I was going to die. I was thinking...would it have killed me to try harder at soccer..." He sniffed loudly, wiped his nose with the back of his hand. "If I'd tried harder since it mattered to Dad so much? I could have tried or pretended to like it. I was thinking, I'm going to die..." Another loud sniff. "And Dad will be glad it's me and not Courtney. He won't miss me... he won't... he won't even notice I'm gone."

"Kevin, you can't mean that, you're not yourself—"

"How can you even think that way—"

"Oh, Kevin—"

Everyone was reacting and talking at once.

"Can you let me finish?" Kevin sucked in a deep breath and let it out slowly. "That's what I was thinking at first. Then I started thinking, you know what?" He wiped his eyes and swallowed hard, determined not to break down again. "I'm going to quit soccer even if I don't lose my toes, and I'm going to be on the swim team, and if you don't like it—well, never mind. Because something happened. Something important. You'll see, Dad. You'll find out I'm not such a loser." He sank back against the pillow, wondering if he should tell them about his experience now or wait until later.

Later, he decided. Besides, with him being in the hospital, they looked like they had enough to worry about. "Dad, did you say coast guard? What happened, exactly? It's all a bit hazy."

They took turns telling him. Around eleven o'clock at night he'd woken up in a panic and gone tearing off in the dinghy. His mother hadn't been able to stop him. She'd called his dad on his cell phone—he and Courtney were still at the concert in Lunenburg—and they'd come home, but Kevin still hadn't. By then it was after midnight. They tried the Nickersons, and when Kevin wasn't there they called the coast guard.

They had found Kevin at one thirty in the morning the previous day, draped over the hull of a dinghy with a broken-down outboard, drifting far from shore. His feet and hands were blue, his toes numb and blistered, his breathing and pulse slow. He was disoriented and barely conscious.

In the coast guard boat he was immediately stripped of his wet clothing and wrapped in a blanket, rushed to a hospital in Shelburne, and treated for hypothermia: warmed IV fluids, warming blankets, several warm-water baths to thaw out his toes and bring his body temperature back to normal.

"So..." Kevin said. "That's it?"

"Isn't that enough?" Courtney teased. "Face it, you're a mess."

"When do I get out of here?"

"Another three days," his mum said. "They want to keep you under observation."

Kevin put his arm over his eyes, overcome by weariness. "Can you guys leave and come back later? I have to tell you something, but first I need to sleep."

He slept for ten hours, vaguely aware of people coming and going, his mum stroking his brow, his dad dozing in the chair and snoring, a nurse taking his temperature, a doctor looking at his chart, Courtney placing a doughnut on the bedside table.

He slept without a sound from Annie's ghost, but he wasn't surprised. She had seen for herself that her precious boy had survived. *That* was the unfinished business. Her needing to know what had happened. For whatever reason, she must have handed Michael to someone when they were still on the *Titanic*. Because she'd needed to put on her life belt or button her boots? Or look for the leather purse she might have dropped?

In the crush of people, she could have been separated from the person holding Michael. She could have been looking for him, not knowing that he was already in a lifeboat. When the bow of the *Titanic* went down and the giant wave swept over the deck, she could have been washed away like so many others. She could have made it to the overturned collapsible, only to be swept away when the funnel crashed into the sea.

However it happened, Annie had died in the water without knowing of Michael's fate. She hadn't known until Kevin went back and showed her. He hadn't changed the outcome. But now her spirit could rest.

Kevin wished she had woken him up from his sleep. A simple *Thank you* would have been nice. *Thanks and good-bye.* She might have said, *See you in the next life...*

Not funny. Though if Zack were there, he would have thought so and laughed. The old Kevin would have, too.

"Well, guys," Kevin said. "I have a theory about the connection between Dad and Angus Seaton."

While in the hospital he'd been trying to figure out the best way to bring up the subject, and now that they were on their way back to Shearwater Point he decided to dive right in. Especially since he was in the backseat of the car and could avoid direct eye contact with his dad.

"That's great, Kevin!" His mother turned in her seat to smile at him. "Is this something you discovered before you went off in the dinghy?"

"Sort of," he lied. "Dad, was your grandmother's name Margaret? And was her last name Dyson before she was married?"

"Right on both counts," he replied. "Did I tell you that?"

"Actually, Miss Dyson told me herself," Kevin said in a half-joking tone. They'd have a hard time figuring that one out. "And Dad, remember you were telling me about your summers on Pender Island, and you said that family was important, because that's like... that's who you are?"

"Yeah, sure I remember." He glanced over his shoulder and gave Kevin a quick smile before turning his attention back to the road. "Why do you ask?"

"Because you're not who you think you are. Actually, none of us are, if my theory is right. So here goes." He spoke quickly, wanting to get it out before anyone could interrupt. "The connection between you and Angus Seaton was your dad, Michael Messenger. *He's* the Michael in the picture frame and it's *his* birth certificate. His mother was Annie. She died when the *Titanic* sank. And when Angus Seaton was on the *Mackay-Bennett* he recovered her body, and he recovered the purse, too, but he kept that and hid it in the box. See? And when Michael was in the lifeboat, you know who was looking after him? Margaret Dyson. And she was going to New York to marry a guy called Messenger. Think about it."

No one spoke. Kevin wasn't surprised. Better they say nothing than make fun of him. They probably thought he was still disoriented.

Reading about the *Titanic*, seeing and hearing the "ghost" (which they never believed anyway), drifting in the Atlantic and suffering from hypothermia—all that put together was bound to affect him.

"Hmm," his mother said after a while. "Interesting theory."

"So how exactly do you 'know' all this, Kevin?" asked Courtney.

"Because..." He hesitated. "I know because the ghost, Annie, took me back to the *Titanic*. I can't explain more than that. But you can check out some websites. I haven't had a chance to look for Margaret Dyson's name on the passenger list, but I bet you anything it'll be there. And for sure you'll find a description of Annie. Under 'unidentified bodies.'"

More silence. After a while Kevin's dad said, "How are your toes? They still hurt? We've got some painkillers if you need them."

"They're fine," Kevin said. Typical Dad, back to the comfort zone of reality. Toes he could handle. Ghosts from the past, not so much. He'd have to, once they were back in Victoria. First thing Kevin planned to do was to go through the boxes above the garage. Somewhere among his grandfather's papers and photographs, he'd find the proof his dad needed. And he'd look at Kevin and admit that he'd been right.

Chapter Thirty

Victoria, B.C.

Kevin stared at the piles of boxes and frowned. Where to start? The bulging cardboard cartons scrawled with *Mess. Stuff*? Or the lidded boxes neatly labeled *Personal Effects of George and Margaret Messenger*?

On the way back from Halifax, he'd suggested that they have Annie's name put on her grave, now that she was no longer unknown. His parents and Courtney had scoffed, saying that a photograph, a birth certificate, and Kevin's "theory" were hardly enough to go on. But they'd jumped at his offer to go through the boxes to see what else might turn up, and had helped move them into the family room. Now, with everyone out shopping, he was on his own.

Personal Effects, he decided, and opened the first box. Photos, photos... same with the second box. Weddings, family gatherings, babies, men in uniform, nothing that couldn't wait for later. If he stopped to look closely he'd never get finished before school started. And that was less than a week away.

In the third box he found what he'd been hoping for—a folder containing legal documents that backed up his theory. At the same time, they made his skin shiver. A theory was one thing. But now he had actual proof!

Margaret Dyson's birth certificate. George Messenger's. Their marriage certificate, June 23, 1912. Best of all, a document dated March 31, 1913, proving that Michael had been adopted by the Messengers of New York City. A document full of "unknowns"—Michael's date and place of birth, the names of his mother and his father—and Kevin could now fill in the blanks. "Wait'll Dad sees this," he said proudly, setting the documents aside where they couldn't be missed.

His heart welled up when he opened the next folder. Yellowed newspaper clippings, some from foreign countries, with the headline **Do You Know This Child?** Photographs of Michael, looking as Kevin remembered. Stories about the "*Titanic* Tot" and the search for his next of kin. The headlines changed as time went on. **Hopes Fade for Titanic Tot**. No longer on the front page. Later still, no headline or article, just a few lines about Michael in the *Notices* sections. Then, on March 5, 1913, Michael was back on the front page. **Happy Ending Imminent for Baby Michael!** The accompanying photo showed a smiling Michael with his parents-to-be.

Kevin brushed away tears and grabbed another box. What more could he possibly find? His fingers flew through letters, greeting cards, photo albums, but all he could think about was the stuff he'd already found. He had to tell someone. When would his parents be home? God, how long did it take to go shopping? And why didn't they ever take their cell phones? Forget Courtney, she'd gone off with friends. He could return Zack's calls. Zack had phoned twice and left messages, but Kevin hadn't picked up, preferring to stick to his task. No point telling Zack, he wouldn't get—

"Oh my God!" he burst out. A diary. Its leather cover embossed with *Margaret Dyson Messenger, 1917*.

Kevin was flipping through the pages when a familiar date caught his eye. *April 15*. From the moment he began to read, he was hooked.

"Hey, Kevin! How's it going?"

Kevin sprang to his feet, startled to see that his parents and sister had come in without his noticing. "You guys won't believe what I found. There's tons more to do and stuff you've got to see, but first you have to read this, like *now*. 'Cause remember I told you about Margaret Dyson on the lifeboat? Well, this is her diary. Here, Dad. Read this part. And read it out loud."

With a bemused look at Kevin, he began.

"*April 15, 1917*

"*There was a memorial service today to mark the fifth anniversary of the sinking of the* Titanic. *I did not attend. Although I was there that fateful night, it wasn't until later that the full effects struck home. At the time, and for the longest time afterward, there was simply too much to do. Primarily, taking care of Baby Michael in the lifeboat. It was a miracle that the little mite survived. Once we were on the* Carpathia *I saw many toddlers and babies reunited with their families and I prayed that Michael's mother or someone else, like the unknown boy, would come forth to claim him. Alas, it did not happen, and I feared that theirs might have been among the bodies I saw floating in the water.*

"*It was not until after George and I were married and settled that I had time to reflect on what had happened. And only then did the horror begin to register. I've been tormented with nightmares these five years, and whenever I see or hear the word* Titanic *I suffer from uncontrollable shaking. At this very moment my fingers shake so that I can barely grasp the pen. George tries to understand but he wasn't there. When we adopted Michael—*"

"Your dad was adopted?" Courtney broke in. "How come you never told us?"

He shrugged. "Does it matter?"

"God, Dad! He was on the *Titanic*!"

"Well, I didn't know that, and neither did he. Or if he did, he never let on." His voice sounded regretful. "Probably thought I wasn't interested. I never cared about family history. Not his, not my mum's, not anybody's..."

"Keep reading, Dad," said Kevin. "You're almost at the good part."

"When we adopted Michael I made George promise never to speak of the tragedy and I have vowed the same, for I do not want Michael troubled by my reaction or by whatever memories his mind might have buried. He is our beloved son and we are determined to make his life a happy one.

"When he is old enough, we'll tell him that he was adopted as a baby. If he asks about his real parents, we'll say that we know nothing about them, and that is the truth.

"There was a 3rd class passenger on the Carpathia *who said she thought Michael's mother was Irish but she could have been mistaken. The boy on the lifeboat..."*

Kevin's dad looked up, an expression of disbelief scrawled across his forehead.

"Don't stop, Dad!" Kevin said. "She's writing about me."

"The boy on the lifeboat who told me that Michael's mother's name was Annie might have been mistaken. I might have been mistaken about the boy. None of the other passengers mentioned him. Could they all have forgotten? There was evidence of such confusion during the Senate inquiry, where witnesses made conflicting statements. I understand how it can happen. The mind confuses the details. We forget some things and remember others. Our dreams and imaginings are mistaken for the truth."

"Well?" said Kevin, breaking the silence that followed.

"That's some find," his dad replied. "What can I say? But I'll tell you one thing. I'm curious to see what else is in these boxes. How about we all chip in? I've ordered pizza for seven o'clock, so we have an hour."

Courtney had already started. "This box is a mess!" she said. "Hundreds of scrapbooks, old notebooks, loose photos—aww! Your baby pictures, Dad. You were such a cutie."

By this time Kevin was halfway through another box. It was hard to stay focused with the others laughing over his dad's childhood photos and, after a fruitless search on his part, he joined in. Seeing his dad as a two-year-old prompted Kevin to bring out the portrait he'd found of Michael at the same age. The resemblance was striking.

"Any more good ones, Kev?" Courtney asked. "We can put them on the mantel."

"You have a look," he said, and turned to the box that his mum was going through. Photos of Dad's summers on Pender Island! Not in a jumble, but organized by year into separate albums. Kevin skipped over the early years and found the ones where his dad was around his age. They showed many of the scenes his dad had talked about—camping with friends, fishing with his dad, rowing with his mum, hamming it up on the float, blowing out candles on his birthday cake, every July 20.

The summer of 1973 was different. After so many father-and-son photos, Kevin couldn't help but notice that in July and August of 1973 the father was absent. "Dad?" he said. "What happened to your dad in the summer of '73? All these pictures are of you and your mum, or you and your friends. Your dad wasn't even there on your birthday."

"He's back in '74, though," Kevin's mum pointed out. "And through to the end of the album. Was he ill in '73, Jim? I don't think you ever mentioned it."

"*That* was the summer he went away," he said. "I was so mad. He went off to New York to be with Grandpa Messenger. He was really sick and then he died, and Dad had to settle his estate and all that, being an only child and my grandmother gone. I ended up having a good enough summer without him, but I was hurt that he missed my birthday. He didn't get back until after school started. Mum and I had to close up the cottage ourselves."

Kevin frowned. Dad had been mad over that?

"Boo-hoo!" Courtney said, voicing Kevin's thoughts. "Talk about self-centered! Your dad probably felt as bad as you did. Worse, since his father had died."

"This is weird…" Kevin began, changing the subject. "This album ends in July 1976. Before the end of the summer, and there isn't the usual birthday party—oh. You would have been sixteen. That's when your mum died. Right?"

"Yeah." His dad gave him a sad smile. "Dad sold the place after that. I was so into soccer I didn't care that much, and I don't think he had the heart to go there on his own." He rose to his feet and stretched. "Enough of this memory stuff. I'm off to pick up the pizza."

With only two days to get ready for school, Kevin had to stop digging into the past and concentrate on the present—registering for swim classes, shopping for school supplies, and catching up with Zack.

They spent a day together, swimming at the Crystal Pool, eating take-out fish 'n' chips at the harbor, and buying stuff at the mall. Afterward, when Zack wanted to hang out at the food court in case any of their friends showed up, Kevin passed. He'd see them soon enough, and the food court was crowded and noisy.

"Never bothered you before," Zack said.

"Well, it does now. Anyway, I've got stuff to do."

As they were walking home, Zack asked about soccer. "You sent me a text saying you were going to quit. Did you tell your dad?"

"I chickened out the first time," Kevin said. "It wasn't until the accident—"

"What accident? You never said anything about an accident."

"The boat flipped over. After that I told Dad I'd had enough soccer. He's okay about it."

"Was it the rowboat, like in the picture you sent?"

"Dory, not rowboat."

"Whatever. How did it flip over? Were you hurt?"

Kevin grimaced. He didn't want to explain. Hadn't meant to bring it up. "Would you believe me if I told you I was on the *Titanic* when she hit the iceberg? And that I met my future grandfather?"

Zack snorted. "In your dreams, Messenger."

"Well, that's why I can't explain about the accident. Tell me about your summer. Did you hear any rumors about the eighth-grade teachers?"

He half-listened as Zack filled him in, laughing and making comments when it seemed appropriate. But most of the time his mind was in the boxes, wondering what the next discovery might be.

The first week back at school, Kevin's class had to write an essay about their summer vacations. The assignment was met with the usual groans, but Kevin, generally the leader in such outbursts, remained silent. He'd written a page before Zack and his other friends had even picked up their pens.

An hour later, when the teacher was asking various kids to read their essays, Kevin tried to look invisible. But the next thing he knew, he was standing in front of the class. He looked at his grinning classmates, half of whom he'd known since first grade, and knew what they were thinking. Kevin the clown, always a source of amusement, he wouldn't let them down.

"This summer I had a near-death experience and met a ghost," he began.

The class erupted with laughter.

"That's enough!" Mr. Ringstrom shouted. He ordered Kevin to sit down. "Don't you know the difference between fiction and nonfiction? I want this garbage rewritten as an essay before the end of the day. Is that clear?"

"Yes, sir." Kevin didn't argue. What was the point?

"Let this be a warning," Mr. Ringstrom added. "I know your reputation for being a jerk, and if you want to get through the year you'd better smarten up. That goes for the rest of you. Got it, Zachary? You're next. Let's see if you followed the instructions."

Kevin folded the papers of his so-called "fiction" and started again. He never should have mentioned the ghost. Of course everybody laughed. It was stupid to think they'd take his account seriously. His goal for the next ten months? Do what the teachers expected and get the job done. The harder he worked at school, the more time he'd have for more important matters. Like swimming. And going through the remaining boxes.

"What was that ghost stuff all about?" Zack asked after school. "Like, what were you *thinking*?"

Kevin shrugged. "I wrote about what happened, like I said before."

"What? That stuff about your grandfather being on the *Titanic*? You're full of it. His name wasn't on the list when we were at the museum, was it?"

"No, and neither was his mother's. But that doesn't mean anything. Some of the third-class passengers got overlooked."

"Yeah, yeah," said Zack. "You want to hang out, play some video games?"

"I can't. Got to sort through some boxes."

"Jeez, Kevin. *Boxes*? What *happened* to you in Halifax?"

"Shearwater Point."

"Whatever! You used to be fun. You used to be a—I don't know."

"A jerk?"

"Well, yeah." He laughed.

"Sorry," Kevin said, "but things aren't so funny anymore. See you tomorrow." He waved and turned the corner for home.

He'd taken the last two boxes to his room when the others were moved to the spare room. "See why I never dealt with this before?" his dad had said. "Now that we've gone through it, what do we do with all this stuff?"

Simple, Kevin thought as he leafed through more of Michael Messenger's papers. They could pick out the best photos, get them digitized—

Suddenly he stopped, his hand frozen on a thin folder labeled *Letter from Angus Seaton*. "Dad!" he yelled. "Mum! Anybody home?"

He took out the letter, put it down, picked it up again, and tried to read. Hands shaking, pulse racing, eyes welling up and blurring the words.

" '*My name is Angus Seaton...*' Oh my God. Angus Seaton. A letter!"
This was it. This was the proof he'd been looking for.

He had to keep moving. He set the table for dinner, made a salad,
put the frozen lasagna into the oven, and read the letter so many times he
almost knew it by heart.

"Finally!" he said, hearing someone in the hall. "Courtney! See this
letter? Where's Mum and Dad?"

"How should I know?" she said. "What's with you?"

"God, I wish they'd get home." He went outside, picked flowers to put
on the table—why, he had no idea—and paced around the house.

At last they arrived. "This is a lovely surprise," his mum said, looking at
the dining room table. "Thank you."

"You think that's a surprise?" He waved the letter. "You won't believe this."

"We're famished," his dad said. "Can't it wait?"

"Nope. Everybody sit down and listen. Don't interrupt. And prepare
to be amazed."

"Shearwater Point
"Shelburne County, Nova Scotia
"August 20, 1973

"To Mr. Michael Messenger:
"My name is Angus Seaton. You may recall I made your acquain-
tance a week ago in Halifax at the Fairview Lawn Cemetery. I go
there now and then to visit my family's graves and the graves of
Titanic victims. You saw me in the Titanic area and struck up a
conversation and when you told me you were a baby on the ship and
your name was Michael and you were adopted by a couple named
Messenger, well, I was shocked to the heart. Because all these years
I believed that Michael was the unknown child the Mackay-Bennett
crew recovered and saw buried. He was fair-haired like the Michael in
the photograph but now that I think about it, the unknown child was a
bit older. I don't know how I could have been wrong but I was. Like I

say, I was shocked and I tried to tell you about your mother and what happened on my part but I had trouble speaking. And so you gave me a card with your name and address and I now have it in mind to write to you so you have the whole story.

"In 1912 I was a seaman on the Mackay-Bennett and we were sent to pick up bodies after the Titanic went down. On April 24, I picked up the body of a young woman and something fell out of her coat and I put it in my pocket. It was a small leather purse. I didn't look inside because at the time it was late and the worst day for bodies and all of us in the cutter, we wanted to get back to the ship before dark, and there was lots going on with so many bodies and where to put them in the cutter.

"I was taking the purse to the duty officer that night when another officer ordered me to go below and secure a stack of bodies because they were loose and rolling around, there was such a pile up of bodies. And after that I was on watch and one thing after another and I forgot about the purse and there were more bodies the next day and the next and when I remembered it was too late. I was afraid of losing my job if it looked like I stole the purse. And the years went by and one day I open it and find a picture frame with photographs and the words Annie and Michael, our precious boy. April 2, 1912.

"You say you loved the Messengers like they were your own kin and I'm glad of that but the reason you were adopted is because no one knew anything about you, because the only thing that would have helped to identify you was the picture frame I kept. So this letter is my confession that I robbed the dead and I kept your birthright and kept you from knowing your true father and mother and relations, whoever they were. What I did is a crime under the law and even though I never went to jail I have been punished. Your mother has seen to that. I suffered years of her torment. I tried to find a way of making atonement and now I can. So Michael Messenger, I am bequeathing to you my property at Shearwater Point, and in the event of your death the *property will go to your heirs. This bequest will come into effect after the death of my only son Myles Frederick Seaton.*

"I have been to my lawyer and made up my Will. And I have met with my son Myles and explained everything and he will honor my bequest to you because he has no attachment to Shearwater Point and no children and enough property of his own.

"After I post this letter I am rowing out past the bay and I will keep rowing until your mother's ghost appears like it always does, only this time I will go with her to the Titanic and I will do what has to be done so that poor girl's spirit can be laid to rest.

"Good luck and God be with you.

"Angus Seaton"

"That's it," Kevin said. He'd looked up now and then during the reading to gauge the others' reactions, and had seen they were much like his own. Shock, disbelief, amazement. In his dad's face now, though, he caught glimpses of anger and hurt. "Dad? You OK?"

"Why didn't he tell me?" he cried, brushing a hand across his eyes. "That letter—damn it, he should have showed me."

"Why?" Courtney said. "People don't have to tell everything. Or *know* everything. Why wouldn't he keep some things to himself?"

"Did he even show my mother? I thought we were close, I thought— forget it."

"The date's August 1973," Kevin reminded him. "Remember, the summer he was away? And when he came back—"

"You're right...I was too busy and that's the way it was. You were right about everything else, too. I don't understand it, but that was some theory you had. You were dead right."

Kevin smiled. Vindication, capital V.

Halfway through September Kevin came home from school and noticed a brochure for kayaking lessons on the kitchen counter. He was looking it over when his dad came in and announced that *he* was thinking of signing up. "What do you think, Kev? Interested in joining me?"

"Are you kidding? Yeah! But I never thought...do you have time on Saturdays? What about soccer?"

"I'm cutting back a bit. You enjoyed the dory so much, why not a kayak? Here's something else I want to show you." He handed Kevin an article printed off the Internet. "I've been thinking of what you said about having Annie's name put on her grave."

"You were? That's great!"

"The thing is, I was searching for information on the identification of bodies and came across this article. It's from a forensic science journal, about a *Titanic* victim, a little boy, who was buried in Halifax as 'the unknown child.' Now he's been identified. In 2008, actually. Thanks to DNA testing."

"Sidney Leslie Goodwin, age 19 months on April 15, 1912," Kevin read. He skimmed over the pages of the article. "Oh man. This is way technical."

"Complicated, right? I thought so, too. Anyway, I got started. Made a call to the Nova Scotia Medical Examiner to find out how to go about it."

"That's awesome, Dad. I didn't think you were that interested."

"I wasn't, to be honest. Now I can't help it. Your enthusiasm must be contagious."

By the end of September, Kevin's family had made copies of all the relevant material and put together a case for opening Annie's grave and exhuming her body. The number of items had swelled since Kevin's initial find, and now included Michael's adoption papers, the pages in Margaret Messenger's diary, and the name *Margaret Dyson* highlighted on the *Titanic*'s list of surviving passengers. It also included Angus Seaton's letter, the purse and its contents, the number assigned to Annie's body, and the coroner's description of her appearance and personal effects.

There was no guarantee that the remains would contain what was needed. That could be a portion of dense bone from an arm or a leg—as little as one-tenth of an ounce would do it—or an unbroken tooth. Any such material could have preserved the DNA that is passed from a mother to all her children. *Mitochondrial* DNA, to be precise. Technical? Complicated? Kevin had had no idea.

Once the material had been sent to Halifax, there was nothing to do but wait.

Kevin threw himself into his schoolwork, swimming lessons, and team practices—he and Zack had made the city team, so had to spend even more time at the pool—and kayaking with his dad. Sunday mornings became his favorite time of the week.

He liked the sessions he was having with his counselor. Given his behavior during the summer, his parents had insisted he go, at least until the new year. He liked having someone to talk to for a whole hour with no chance of being interrupted. Strange thing was, he was starting to have good talks with his dad. Mostly while they were kayaking.

He saw Zack at school and at swimming, but apart from that, not so much.

Every day he rushed home to see if there was any news from Halifax. The answer was always the same. Until finally, in early December, they received word that permission had been granted. The grave would be opened. All they needed to do was provide a blood sample from Kevin's dad so that his DNA could be compared with Annie's—in the event the exhumation was successful.

That done, there was nothing more to do but wait. "Don't get your hopes up" became a family refrain.

In the new year, whenever he had time to spare, Kevin looked into various genealogical sites, searching for information on his great-grandfather John Edward Collins. His winter project.

Several months later they heard that during a partial exhumation of the body, a team of forensic researchers had recovered a tooth and a small portion of an arm bone. The DNA obtained from these fragments matched that of Kevin's dad, and confirmed that the remains were those of Annie McConnell.

Chapter 31

Halifax, Nova Scotia, July 8, 2011

In Memory of Annie McConnell
Died April 15, 1912
Age 17
Devoted mother of Michael McConnell Messenger

Kevin rearranged the flowers at the foot of the gravestone to make room for the new ones he'd brought. He'd gotten up before the others, set off on an early morning run, and made it all the way from downtown Halifax to the Fairview Lawn Cemetery. This was his last chance to visit the cemetery. In a couple of hours they'd be leaving for Shearwater Point.

The flowers had been a lucky find. He'd stopped at a store for a cold drink, and bought the last bunch available. A couple of days old, but still. It was something you did when you went to a cemetery.

Since the sinking of the *Titanic*, Annie's gravestone had been like those of the other unidentified victims. A black granite block marked with a number and the date of her death. Now the gravestone bore her name, her age, and an inscription. She would not be forgotten.

On a visit to the Maritime Museum, Kevin had asked about the bags of personal effects that had been left unclaimed. He'd been thinking of Annie's copper-wire ring, hoping that the bags might still be available to relatives. Not a chance. Most of the unclaimed bags had been sent to the White Star office in New York but had long since disappeared. As had a small number of bags stored in Halifax.

Kevin wondered if John Collins, Michael's father, had given Annie the ring. Had it been a promise of sorts? He liked to think so—though he would never admit to such a romantic notion. As for Annie being his *great-grandmother* . . . it was beyond awesome. Beyond comprehension. He hoped she was resting easy in the spirit world.

He sat on the grass, in no hurry to get back to the hotel, content to stay awhile and let his mind wander.

The day after their arrival in Halifax, his family had held a small memorial service at Annie's new gravestone. The victims of the *Titanic* were in a separate area of the cemetery, their gravestones laid out in rows that curved gently up a slope, appearing like the hull of a ship. After placing flowers on Annie's grave, they'd walked by each of the one hundred twenty-one gravestones, pausing while Kevin's mum read information about the person that she and Kevin had found on a website. It was a small sampling of the types of passengers and crew who'd been on board—those whose bodies had been picked up by the *Mackay-Bennett* or one of the other recovery ships. Trimmers, greasers, firemen, a vegetable cook, waiters, stewards, an assistant clothes presser, a pantry-man, second- and third-class passengers.

Kevin looked at his watch and realized it was almost time to head back to the hotel. By evening they'd be at Shearwater Point. It would be good to see Jarrett again, and Mrs. Nickerson. She was going to be stunned by the rest of the Angus Seaton story. And wait till she heard about Michael.

Before leaving the cemetery, Kevin had one other grave to visit.

He left the *Titanic* section, strolled past the graves of those who had died in the Halifax Explosion, and eventually found his way to a simple stone plaque that marked the grave of Angus Seaton.

"Hey, Angus," he said. He lowered his voice, feeling self-conscious even though he was alone. "The store was out of flowers, but I brought a couple from Annie's grave. You're probably not big on flowers anyway.

"There's a few things I have to tell you. Annie's got a name on her grave now. In time for the hundredth anniversary of the *Titanic*. Isn't that cool? I know she gave you a rough time. Me too.

"Another thing . . . well, I just want to say thanks. It was terrible what you and the crew had to do, but my family's grateful. I'm grateful. And thanks for writing the letter to Michael. I'm glad you met him. Oh, and I got your wreck-wood box repaired. It's almost as good as new, and I promise I'll take care of it.

"So . . . that's it for now. God be with you, Angus. And with Annie and with everybody else who lies here."

Before leaving the cemetery, Kevin paused at the *Titanic* graves to take a last look around. It was a good place to think, there among the ghosts. But he'd lingered too long.

Overcome with emotion, he hurried on. "See you, Annie," he said, waving as he passed her grave.

He was certain she whispered something in return.

On second thought, it must have been the wind.

He hoped it was the wind.

Author's Note

The story of the *Titanic* is well known, and the facts and fiction surrounding her ill-fated voyage have never ceased to enthrall. Public interest will be fueled even further in 2012, as the sinking of the *Titanic* marks its 100th anniversary.

A lesser-known aspect of the *Titanic* story is its connection to Halifax, Nova Scotia. Few people know that it fell on Canadian ships to recover victims' bodies and take them to Halifax. Many were subsequently identified, claimed by next of kin, and transported for burial. For 150 victims, both unidentified and identified, their final resting place was Halifax (in the Protestant Fairview Lawn Cemetery, the Catholic Mount Olivet, or the Jewish cemetery, Baron de Hirsch). They are the largest number of *Titanic* victims buried together anywhere in the world.

I hadn't planned to write a book based on the *Titanic*, especially after being immersed in the writing of *No Safe Harbour*, a novel set during the explosion that shattered Halifax on December 6, 1917. This disaster—the largest man-made explosion in history until the dropping of the atomic bomb in 1945—was caused when the *Mont-Blanc*, a steamer carrying munitions, collided with another ship in the Narrows of Halifax Harbour.

Almost at once the *Mont-Blanc* was on fire. The crew and pilot, aware of the danger, took to the lifeboats and rowed to safety as the abandoned ship drifted toward a pier at the north end of the harbor. The fiery spectacle drew crowds of onlookers, unaware that they were watching a floating bomb.

Twenty minutes after the collision, the *Mont-Blanc* exploded. The force blasted the 3,000-ton ship into a spray of metallic fragments and instantly took the lives of 1,600 people. Hundreds more perished in the tsunami and fires that followed. Although the recovery and identification of some 2,000 victims was a monumental undertaking, the majority of victims were identified—thanks to a system developed five years earlier by Dr. John Henry Barnstead, the Deputy Registrar of Deaths in Halifax at the time of the *Titanic*'s sinking.

I was intrigued by Dr. Barnstead's skillfully improvised system, particularly in its meticulous recording of details. In a way, this further connection between Halifax and the *Titanic* took me from one disaster to another.

The system involved numbering each body as it was taken from the sea and placing personal effects in canvas mortuary bags, each bag bearing the same number as the body. Details were noted as to the approximate age, facial features, tattoos, clothing, jewelry—not even the smallest detail was overlooked.

Thanks to these records and DNA testing, scientists such as pathologists and anthropologists from American and Canadian institutions have been able to put names on some previously unidentified *Titanic* graves. In 2008, for example, the "unknown child" buried by the crew of the *Mackay-Bennett* was identified as Sidney Leslie Goodwin. His body had previously been identified as that of a thirteen-month-old Finnish child, but the size of a pair of shoes belonging to Body No. 4 raised the question, how could the shoes have remained on the Finnish child's small feet? The DNA confirmed that the body was that of nineteen-month-old Sidney. His brown shoes are now in the collection of the Maritime Museum of the Atlantic.

Dr. Barnstead's system helped to identify many of the *Titanic* victims recovered by the *Mackay-Bennett* and the three other recovery ships. Of the 328 bodies eventually recovered, 119 were buried at sea, the majority (116) by the *Mackay-Bennett*.

Why so many? As the first vessel to reach the disaster site, the *Mackay-Bennett* was unprepared to keep and preserve the large number of bodies that were found. With coffins for 125, embalming fluid for 70, a ton of ice in the hold, and a limited amount of canvas, the supplies on board were clearly inadequate. Especially when fifty-one bodies were recovered on the first day alone.

Captain Larnder, who made the decision to conduct sea burials, had other factors to consider. How long would his crew be required to stay at the grim task? How many bodies would ultimately be recovered? How long could he safely carry a large number of dead? And, given the bad weather, how long would it take to return to Halifax? As for *which* bodies would be buried at sea, determining factors included a lack of personal effects to assist in identification, and the victim's apparent social class, as indicated by their clothing. The deaths of prominent and wealthy passengers could give rise to legal problems involving inheritance and insurance. Such victims were therefore embalmed as quickly as possible and placed in coffins.

Many of those buried at sea were members of the *Titanic*'s crew. For seafaring men, a sea burial was regarded as fitting and appropriate. Even if their bodies were taken to Halifax, there was little hope that their families could afford to transport them home for burial. The same went for bodies of third-class passengers.

Sea burials were held on the *Mackay-Bennett*'s first two days at the site and again on the fourth, after a passing ship supplied her with more canvas. From then on, there were no further burials at sea.

My interest in the identification system, combined with the role played by Canadian crews in recovering bodies, gave rise to the spark of an idea and to several "What if..." questions concerning the effects this experience would have had on the crew, the possibility of mistaken identity, and the consequences of not following the system to the letter.

Further ideas were inspired by contemporary accounts and coroners' files, the *Titanic* exhibit in the Maritime Museum of the Atlantic where I discovered the sailor's tradition of carving wreck wood, the "back in time" flavor of the traveling exhibit *Titanic: The Artifact Exhibition,* and the *Titanic* section of the Fairview Lawn Cemetery in Halifax. Being there in the stillness of an early morning was a moving experience.

Acknowledgments

Thanks to Janet MacDonald, Manager of Learning & the Visitor Experience at the Royal BC Museum; Dan Conlin, Curator of Marine History at the Maritime Museum of the Atlantic; Garry D. Shutlak, Senior Reference Archivist of Nova Scotia Archives and Records Management; Alan Ruffman, Honorary Research Associate in the Earth Sciences department at Dalhousie University in Halfiax, Nova Scotia and author of *Titanic Remembered: The Unsinkable Ship* and *Halifax;* my trusted editors Sandy Bogart Johnston of Scholastic Canada and Julie Amper of Holiday House, for their invaluable insights and comments; and my husband Patrick, for tossing me a life preserver on more than one occasion.